Pretend All Your
LIFE

Pretend All Your
LIFE

Joseph Mackin

THE PERMANENT PRESS
Sag Harbor, NY 11963

For information, address:
    The Permanent Press
    4170 Noyac Road
    Sag Harbor, NY 11963
    www.thepermanentpress.com

Library of Congress Cataloging-in-Publication Data

    Mackin, Joseph.
        Pretend all your life / Joseph Mackin.
            p. cm.
        ISBN-13: 978-1-57962-196-4 (alk. paper)
        ISBN-10: 1-57962-196-1 (alk. paper)
            1. Plastic surgeons—Fiction. 2. Identity (Psychology)—Fiction.
        3. New York (City)—Fiction. I. Title.

    PS3613.A27344P74 2010
    813'.6—dc22   2009044495

Printed in the United States of America.

For my mother and father,

And for Mary, the one and only

"How with this rage shall beauty hold a plea?"

—Shakespeare, Sonnet LXV

ONE

Richard Gallin, plastic surgeon to Broadway stars and cab-drivers, senators and mafiosi—indeed, anyone with a need—halted abruptly in the center of his marble-floored East Side waiting room, humming a little. Gallin owned, among much else, three homes, his own medical practice, an impressive collection of tribal art and even a large second-rate painting by a Dutch old master. He was rich, or so it seemed. But what stopped him in his tracks was not all that he possessed but a nagging apprehension of his losses.

Office hours had begun. And though Gallin was dressed in a beautifully tailored suit, his horny yellow feet were bare against the marble. He looked haphazard, disturbing Janine, who gazed at him from her desk. The shoelessness signaled to her that he was still half-in, half-out. It was a state, she knew, in which he could no longer afford to linger.

Yet Gallin, formerly a model of noble American avarice, found this new state liberating. It was an indulgence to be afflicted, to be off-balance, to be unsure. He was having trouble, frankly, bringing himself around to his old hungers.

Heavy and still—so rare for a man who had hustled his life away—he considered his situation. Once again his soft surgery schedule wouldn't square with the monthly nut he had let grow so wildly during the twilight of the Clinton years, when blue skies had seemed the permanent fiscal forecast. Now his creditors were pressing on him. For three straight months he'd had to siphon cash from his safe to meet his obligations. But the stacks in that sleek steel chamber, previously a large component of his pride, were dwindling. For years whenever patients paid in cash he'd stashed it away. Cash, the king: borough girls wanting pouty lips came in with rolls of saved-up twenties, strippers reinvesting a week's lewd take in a cup size, doormen after the holidays with their lovehandles and their Christmas loot. It was a good racket. Gallin's services were virtually invisible to the IRS. In the years before September 11th, he'd been able to sock away half-a-million clean.

But a racket was only as good as you swung it. More than half the reserve was now gone, swallowed up by bills for the ravenous life he'd purchased earlier. What was left of the money, if nothing changed, would buy another three months tops. After that he'd have to start divesting.

Every morning Gallin told himself that a couple of strong weeks in the O.R. would stop the financial hemorrhage. And this was true: the money could come in quickly. But sorrow blocked him—and he couldn't find a way to work. Standing there now, the cool floor soothing his soles, he wondered how much more loss he could take.

"Dr. Gallin?"

Janine's voice rose gingerly to his ear.

He walked toward her in the reception area, a trail of moist footprints vanishing in his wake. In his hand he held a West African tribal mask. Delivered that morning, the piece was a strong addition to his collection—a mahogany face with sliced-out Asiatic eyes and rude starburst carvings on the cheeks. Gallin's thumb poked absently through its perfectly circular mouth. He'd bought the mask a week earlier from an online auction in London. Running out of money he bought things.

Peering through the window onto 73rd Street, Gallin noted the ongoing construction. The house across the street was being gutted. Two men stood in front of it drinking coffee and pointing while others lugged heavy equipment around them. Annie and Janine, Gallin's receptionist and patient coordinator, busied their hands. He noticed a small American flag decal that Janine had affixed to the top of the windowpane. It was backwards, its stars in the upper right hand corner. Flags were everywhere now. Across the street one canopied the bed of a mason's pickup. Another was

10

painted freestyle on the side of an electrician's van. Old Glory unfurled from condo windows, draped from lampposts, flew from taxi antennas. New York was never so red, white and blue.

"Any calls?" he asked.

"Yes, four, Dr. Gallin," Janine answered. "All for directions. We're going to be busy Monday."

Janine Russo had worked as Gallin's patient coordinator for fourteen years. She scheduled his surgeries, handled the payments. She was loyal and energetic, an upriver swimmer of the first order. She was also a religious woman, a believer. Lately, of course, she had been praying more than usual. Nearly everyone had. She prayed especially for Gallin, being gravely sorry for his loss and knowing that prayer was a skill he lacked.

The phone rang.

"Ooop, there's another one," Janine said gaily.

She reached for it but Annie, the younger woman—a pretty but incompetent Brooklyn neighbor of Janine's, come to her job through the latter's kindness—grabbed it before it completed a ring. She was anxious. They both were. They were trying hard to keep Gallin's moribund plastic surgery practice—and their own jobs—alive. The digital gurgle of the phone sounded to their ears like a slot machine paying off. Gallin averaged eight-thousand dollars per improvement these days. He performed anything from liposuction to breast augmentation to eyelid surgery to calf implants. He made lips bigger, thighs smaller, noses slimmer and dreams come true. A year ago, he was doing seven, eight, nine procedures a week. His practice was cooking. But now he was down to one or two.

On the line another person wanted directions from the 6-train. Annie began to recite them with exaggerated precision, as much for her lingering boss as for the caller. "You just take it to 77th Street," she said, "and we're just four blocks away. Yes. Just walk down Lex to 73rd and we're on the corner of Park Avenue . . . Right, Park Avenue—"

Gallin stepped back toward the stairs to his office. He was a tall man with large features—a straight prominent prow of a nose,

11

a serious chin, long elaborate hands. He had fleshy poetic earlobes that retained, it seemed, drops from the saddest things he'd heard.

"Dr. Gallin?" Janine said in her gentle, interruptive voice. "There was one other call. That man from *New York* magazine, the writer who called last week—he called again. He's called a few times now saying the same thing."

Turning back to answer, Gallin realized that the American flag decal wasn't backwards at all. The stars could be on either side. Looked at in three dimensions, the placement of the stars depended on where you stood, how the wind blew. It was only in pictures, he realized, that the stars were always on the left.

"A Mr. Adams?" Janine queried.

"Adams?" Gallin answered. "Oh, right."

"Yes, Nick Adams," she replied. "He says he covers crime for *New York* magazine. Is he joking? Do you know him? He says you know him."

If Gallin could cure her of anything, it would be gum chewing.

"No. Well, yes and no. I don't know what he covers. But I believe he does work for the magazine," he said.

Gallin had himself taken strange calls from Adams over the last couple of months. The man had seemed angry about something—what, he wouldn't say—but more or less harmless. Gallin, however, was wary of journalists as a rule: an angry pen could turn a mundane detail malicious with little effort. And publishers encouraged it. Even the smallest unfavorable mention of Gallin in a prominent magazine like *New York* would be difficult to overcome. A cover story, if this Adams somehow managed to scrape up something real, would ruin him.

"He says it's in your interest to call him," Janine said. "Your *best* interest, he says, in this threatening way."

It irked Gallin that in any conversation with Janine, her pink gum slid out to the tip of her tongue and flitted as she spoke. That he became so irritated by this bothered him even more, for against the backdrop of his current troubles such a thing shouldn't even register. Maniacs were razing skyscrapers, civilization had a puncture wound, and yet Janine's gum-smacking still galled.

"He keeps asking if I know what an exposé is," she continued. "That's what he says he's writing. An exposé about you."

"I'll call him."

Gallin took the message from her and put it in his pocket.

"Thank you," he said.

"I *know* what an exposé is," Janine continued. "Then he starts in with 'do you know what kind of man you're working for?' And blah, blah, blah. He sounds crazy, I swear."

Janine would read, of course, an exposé of Gallin more hungrily than anyone. At the same time, she wouldn't want one written.

"I tell him, Dr. G.," she said, her ire up, "*yes I know* what kind of man I'm working for—thank you very much."

"It's nothing to worry about," Gallin said.

"Should I just hang up on him?"

"No, no, please keep taking messages. Be cordial. I'm sorry you have to deal with him but be cordial to anyone who calls."

"Well, yeah, I know. We are. We always are," she said.

Upstairs Gallin dropped the mask onto his large leather-topped desk, where it joined in a crude melee for surface area amidst a modern miscellany: patient records, nude photographs, phone messages, insurance forms, Coke cans, auction catalogues, magazines. With these were yesterday's unfinished scotch and a dozen roses dying in a vase.

The office was a considered room, meant to impress—a J.P. Morgan-style study that started with a floor of gleaming cherry wood and a large intricate Persian carpet. Antique globes from different eras lined the walls in stands. Recessed bookshelves climbed marvelously to the ceiling. These held enormous volumes of austere-looking medical titles, books on astronomy, cartography, game theory and economics, first editions of important American novels, embossed gilt-detailed Dickens and Tolstoy and Proust, the collected Shakespeare. The effect tended to intimidate patients, who during consultations were quick to give themselves over to such a learned physician. Also keeping the Bard company on the shelves were Gallin's own, decidedly not austere, soft-covered books on plastic surgery. Four of them so far, each a moderate commercial success, adorned with photos of beautiful women the author had never met.

Gallin sat at his computer and fed in his password. Beyond the wall, the townhouse elevator grumbled to a stop. He empathized with its arthritic groan, a mechanical version of an old man's grief. Then he heard the excited patter of dog paws, eight of them, the nails clicking and sliding on the floor, making the sound of grade-school tap dancers bolting the stage after a number. In a blond burst, Gallin's loose-mopped Wheaten Terriers tumbled into the office, seemingly attached at the shoulders—a floppy, two-headed bundle.

"Hellooooopuppies, hellooodoggies. My doggies, my doggies, my doggies," their master sang in a familiar refrain that the dogs met with leaps, licks, and convulsing. These dogs brought the troubled man joy. "Give-me-kisses. Give me kisses—what are you doing, where are you going, what are you doing my doggies?"

Andrea stood in the doorway holding their leashes. She looked petulant, wronged, impatient. Gallin glanced over at her. So she decided to get out of bed, he grumbled to himself. The dogs laid themselves, panting and delighted, at his feet.

"I'm taking them to Woodbrook, Richard."

Gallin looked straight ahead at the computer monitor, waiting for it to produce its magic. The surgeon didn't know what form his information took after he typed it in, how it was encrypted, delivered, or decoded. Nor could he grasp precisely how the myriad networks connected, or how this mysterious collaboration brought the Internet home to his screen. But he was deeply moved by the audacity of it. One of the few truly extraordinary inventions, he believed. Such broad application—it couldn't be exaggerated. He would love to know how it worked. Someone should make up a song about it, like they had for the body—with the shin bone connecting to the ankle bone, the ankle bone connecting to the . . .

Perhaps he could write the song, he thought.

"You're not taking them, Andrea," he barked without looking at her. "I'm not going to the country this weekend and they're staying with me."

He was surprised to hear he wasn't going; until that moment he'd intended to jump in his car directly following that afternoon's breast augmentation. He'd already called the garage asking them to have the car ready. Suddenly Gallin felt a little confused: it happened—and he hated it—whenever he said things without first knowing he was going to say them. Recently it happened more often.

He was pissed at Andrea, generally for a thousand reasons, but specifically because he'd wanted sex the night before and she'd resisted. Coy about it, too, teasing, holding her heavy breasts out to him, cupping them underneath in her hands, saying they felt *so swollen*, did they look swollen? "Feel, do they feel swollen to you?" she'd asked.

They'd felt good, good and ripe, when he touched them. And heavy enough so that they were a thing unto themselves: her tits. Beautiful, physical: somehow separate from the whole. But when he moved his hand down between her legs, excited to feel the patch of stubble where she shaved, she said, "C'mon, Richard, let's not. Let's wait until the weekend."

What made it worse was that he understood it. Too frequently he'd slept with Andrea in the city on a Thursday night and found himself in the country with her on the weekend drained of any attention to pay. She was saying attention must be paid. He got it.

All the same, though, if she wasn't going to open up, then he sincerely wished she'd go home to her own place at night and not stay in his bed feeling her ripe tits and cooing.

"Do you hear me, Andrea? They're staying here."

"You told me not an hour ago you were going to Woodbrook to shoot on Saturday with Fred. Did you cancel it?"

"No. Not yet. I'm going to call him when I'm not stuck—when I'm not stuck talking to you anymore." He considered how juvenile he sounded; he didn't care. His eyes remained fixed on the screen. Presto! *Aleach,* his password, had gone off and returned with the Internet. His monitor filled with the illuminated news of the day. It would be tough, he thought, writing the Internet song. Repetitive, boring probably.

"I'm busy, Andrea. I've got a situation I need to figure out how to take care of. I've got a touch-up on a nose this morning. I'm doing breasts this afternoon. I don't have time to—"

"We rsvp'd to Donnie and June's thing for Saturday night, Richard. We should go."

"Andrea, you're not listening to me, dear." His voice rose. "I've got to take care of things here and I've got this woman coming on Sunday to look at the new mask. All the masks, in fact. I've got too much to do."

"What woman?" She shifted onto her right hip, piqued. Then she crouched. "C'mere, Barney," she called to the dog in a loud whisper, sexy and sad, almost teary. "C'mere. Good baby."

She jiggled the leash. One dog came.

Gallin still did not turn toward her. "It doesn't matter what woman. A curator. Used to be at the Met. She's a hundred, I think. She's a fucking hundred, for god's sake." Gallin had no clue as to the woman's age. He simply wished he hadn't mentioned her. Now in making her an old lady he took the path of least resistance. Who could be jealous of a hundred-year-old woman? Andrea let it go.

He clicked a few more times with the mouse, rapidly. A photo of knot-bearded Arabs, prisoners in shackles, on their way to Cuba. They looked defiant. But they had to be scared. They oughta be, he thought.

"Richard, listen to me. You have to begin to socialize again. There's supposed to be some kind of normalcy. People are worried about you."

He considered that simply knowing Andrea, let alone sleeping with her, was a horrible cosmic accident. A disaster.

"Good," he said, "they oughta be worried. They oughta worry about themselves, too. Everybody ought to worry."

Another mouse click. A photo taken a year earlier of the board of directors of Enron, the bankrupt behemoth. 'Smiling for the camera, Aspen, Colorado,' it read. Gallin thought: there is confusion about what evil is.

"Richard," Andrea started and stopped, unsure how to proceed.

She hugged Barney, rubbing her face in his golden coat, holding him close even as the dog, perhaps sensing her neediness, craved release. Andrea had wanted desperately to make the relationship with Richard work, but she was failing. More and more she was perplexed and sad about ending up so far from where she thought she'd go in life, from what she'd hoped for in her fragrant silky early dreams—dreams of love and of mattering.

Yet despite her efforts she'd missed her mark. No marriage, no children. Regret collected in her like kitchen grease till it was solid and clogged her heart. Finally, she was all want and no give.

She even envied the dogs, the gorgeously dependent dogs, wishing more than once that someone would come with *her* leash to take her out. Where was her keeper? Lately she felt panic pricking the backs of her eyes. She took codeine for it.

"Richard, it's been four months. Things are settling, right? I don't mean to be crude but Kiran got her money. She's going to be okay."

Kiran was Bernardo's widowed wife. Bernardo was Gallin's only son, killed in the World Trade Center. "You need to start—"

"I don't need to start anything! If anything, I need to finish some things. Like this. Like this relationship."

"Let's not talk about this right now, Richard. I just want to know if I can take the dogs."

Gallin was anxious for the morning sun to rise above the rooftops across 73rd Street. He craved the warmth. A night chill lingered in the office, whose old windows, beautiful but inefficient, let the cold seep in as carelessly as skin let in disease. The façade of Gallin's house was protected from change by the city landmark commission. Its antique, draughty fenestration couldn't be replaced. Progress be damned. But preservation, so well meaning, was really a losing game. Ultimately it was impossible. The sun should be up above those roofs already, he thought. Gallin hated to wait. How many people have waited for the sun. And for every one a day it doesn't come.

17

"Then when? When will we talk about it? You tell me that."

"Calm down, Richard. You're scaring the dogs. You're scaring me. I don't want—"

"You oughta be scared."

She recognized how tight he was wound this morning and she was tired of it. She was tired, too, from barely sleeping, from keeping herself all cramped up at night, shutting him off and yet still being with him. It confused her body. She decided to try something she'd been considering.

On television that week she'd watched a psychiatrist talking about grief. The man had convinced her of certain things. *"Facts!"* he bellowed at the beautiful, permanently astonished TV hostess. Bald and short, paunchy with protruding egg-like eyes—the strange man seemed to possess a sort of folk wisdom. He wore a plaid flannel shirt with a black-knit necktie, and he looked exactly like he didn't give a shit what anybody thought about him. "State plain facts. Bang-Bang-Bang," he yelled. "Facts can jar someone out of their bitterness. The truth is our medicine!"

He beat a little bongo drum he had on his lap after each pronouncement. To Andrea, he seemed brave. The audience went wild for him. "Trooooth!" they yelled out, declaiming for honesty, spraying spit on the people in front of them. "Trooooth!"

The little man smiled and beat his drum.

Crouched now in the doorway, Andrea was silent. Suddenly, she let Barney go and stood up, taking two purposeful steps into the room. The considerable heels of her black boots punctuated her gait, lent her authority. She stood only ten feet from where he sat at his computer, clicking link after link—the scope of the Internet was astounding.

She tried it.

"Richard, Bernardo's dead. Your son Bernardo was killed in a tragedy. Everybody lost something but you lost more. More than most. You loved him. And maybe there was some unresolved— well, stuff. But now you're not helping anybody with this, this—"

She was not going to cry. That would ruin it, the TV shrink had said. Those were facts, plain facts, she invoked. *Bang-bang-bang.*

She bit her bottom lip, felt her nostrils flare, her eyes redden and puff; they burned around the edges. She wished for a drum, something to bang along to the rhythm of the truth she told. She almost punched her palm. She wondered how the face she showed, contorted by a dumb determination not to cry, could possibly be any better, any more dignified, than tears.

Gallin took a deep breath. He double-clicked on something he wanted to see. On-screen the clip began to load. He appreciated Andrea, he did: for her trying, her candor, her petite version of courage. In fact, her words now were similar to those he often uttered to himself—that he should somehow get over it, in popular parlance. And he felt pity for her too—because he understood that she needed him to take some pressure off her, to exonerate her. She needed release from the torment of not feeling bereft enough, for being undevastated by what had happened. Poor thing, he thought.

Yet even knowing all this he was still angry with her, for he suspected she had learned her new tactic—this confrontational style—from a dubious source. He guessed she'd been encouraged in it by some supposedly mutual friend of theirs, someone who Gallin surely wanted nowhere near his business. Try this, he could hear any number of scheming voices saying. Former friends of his. The same ones probably who were shooting off their mouths to that fucker Adams. It was easy to imagine. Lately, Gallin couldn't get near a man without getting up his nose the stench of the man's failure—his suppurating compromises, his dead passions and secret perversions. Everybody reeked.

But couldn't Andrea have arrived at this on her own? Wanting to believe it, he couldn't. The approach was too direct for her. She would not have conjured it. Andrea was hard. She was determined. She was not easily defeated—but she did not meet things head-on. And she was not original.

Still, Gallin thought, why punish yourself? Why not go to the country? Get out of the city? Do some shooting, run the dogs? These were wholesome things. He should do them. He would forgive her.

19

"C'mere," he said, swiveling his chair toward where she stood.

He didn't want to look too closely. He didn't want to be forced to consider her, not the whole of her. He wanted her coming toward him only as this caring soul, the bare purity of her emotional outreach alone, disembodied, without her swollen tits even. Yet he was not blind. She was a body. A light crescent of mucus glistened under her nose; she wiped it away with the loose silk cuff of her sleeve, sniffling. Beckoned, she walked toward him. She stood between his knees and he reached between hers and felt the slight, sexy bow in her legs. She was holding back great sheets of tears; he felt powerful to have produced such emotion in her.

The sun leapt up over the roofs across the street. The latticework on Gallin's century-old townhouse windows ordered the winter light into gorgeous golden diamonds on the floor. She bent over him. Her tongue darted into his mouth, surprising him. She reached and cupped him in his crotch: and life sprang up there under her touch. The sun, this—everything was rising. He felt a big electric C draw itself inside him, starting at his eyes, dropping to his tongue, curving down through his spine, and signing itself off with an upward flourish in his pants.

The video, fully transferred, began to play on his monitor. Putting his cheek on Andrea's ribs, he looked behind her at the 30-second clip. It was shot the night before. A fight in Atlantic City, a featherweight—a kid with only nine career bouts—had killed his opponent with a right hook. Killed him dead in the ring. Columnists quivered with sanctimony. The Sweet Science, they wrote, was an abomination. Primitive, Neanderthal. Men should be prohibited from fighting for money, they wrote. Ha, Gallin thought—that's the funniest thing in the world. Abolish the sport, they wrote. Evolve, they pleaded.

Gallin just wanted to see the punch.

TWO

That noon Gallin devoured a salmon sandwich with garlic aioli that Annie put silently atop a pile of magazines on his desk. He ate too fast—always did—and paged absently through the gossip columns of the *New York Post*. A little gas escaped him; he fidgeted; he hoped it would be odorless. The boldface names on the greasy page were like traffic lights, green ones. He drove right through them.

A few years back Gallin had been fascinated by the chronicle in these pages of the pop star Prince's quest to change his name to a graphic symbol. It became a story in the real news too—everyone suckers for celebrity—where it borrowed the guise of ethical quandary. The debate concerned who rightfully owned the name Prince—whether its legal proprietor was the little man himself or the large music corporation that held him under contract. Even Tom Brokaw opined, with basso Midwestern gravity, on the nightly news about the "future of identity in our rapidly changing world." But his weary speculation on the subject was eclipsed by the competing footage shown behind him of the chiffon-cloaked, motorcycle-humping, candy-colored rock star riding into the night with a blonde movie star on the back of his bike.

The future of identity stood no chance against the image.

But whereas in the *Times* and other allegedly high-minded media the story enjoyed only momentary light, the gossip pages gave it continual life. Indeed, the tabloids had great fun deciding what to call the diminutive, freshly de-monikered rocker—some even ran contests—before finally anointing him *The Artist Formerly Known as Prince*. This quickly became simply *The Artist*. Not Leonardo or Michelangelo or Picasso but Prince became *the*

21

artist. Gallin was impressed. His interest in legends had always been keen. How did some ascend while others languished? What set people apart? He used to like those fur coat ads that asked: *What becomes a legend most?* Gallin was always trying to understand how some people got to live beyond their time.

No gossip item since the Prince affair had interested him as much. The current crop of celebrities lacked glamour, substance. Even the word—celebrity—felt brittle. Those old fur ads featured Bette Davis, Judy Garland, Marlene Dietrich—women from the firmament. Not celebrities but stars. Times change. Gallin bit a pickle, but it had no flavor and he fired it into the copper-plated can under his desk. It made a satisfying thunk. Can't even get a good pickle in New York, he thought. Sad fucking state.

He headed over to Lexington and caught a cab. The day had warmed considerably and he wore only his suit jacket against the weather. The blue sky hosted a shy wind and the sun shone with a faded grandfatherly passion. Inside, the cab reeked of incense, a maudlin perfume that licked at the back of his throat. He closed his eyes and felt along the door blindly to lower the window. His eyes were already tired. During the night, frustrated by Andrea, he'd tossed like an addict. When he'd finally slept, there was a garish dream about a building rising out of downtown, rising so high and fast that the people on the moon—there was a community of people living on the moon—were afraid the building would poke into its orbit. He woke to a chorus of moon people yelling *wake up earth, wake up earth!* Glass buildings and the moon: Gallin was furious at his mind for lacking subtlety. What kind of unconscious must I have, he asked himself: am I so dull I'm damned to this? What a bunch of junk are dreams, he thought.

He alighted from the cab in front of a Foot Locker store. He'd begun recently to take a good swift walk after his lunch and, though the exercise was welcome, it had put a rotten strain on his knees and feet. Ordinarily, he tried to avoid the type of national chain store in front of which he now stood. He took personally the depersonalization they dispatched; he felt menaced by it—it was a thief of dignity. But the chain store in America was the only option left for certain types of goods—and athletic shoes were one. Inside, multicolored moonboots climbed the walls on pedestals, ordered in some arcane post-modern hierarchy, the code of which Gallin couldn't crack. Some looked like bowling shoes (or as they used to look—what did they look like now, bowling shoes?), some were all plastic, some zippered up the instep instead of lacing, and others were like slippers, with no laces or zippers at all, perhaps for people who confused athletics with making coffee or taking out the trash.

Three young salespeople lingered by the cash register, talking to each other. They wore black-and-white striped referee uniforms. Gallin couldn't at first make out the conversation between the two male salesmen, but he could hear its tenor: heated, he thought. Moving closer, discreetly, he saw clearly there was tension between the two young men—boys really—and the girl was moving away from it. The boys were in each other's faces.

"Naw, Michael da man," said one. He was tall—taller by five inches—black, skinny, about twenty-two. His thick eyebrows, knitted low, gave him an unfortunate appearance of dimwittedness. It was a shame, Gallin thought, because to have low thick eyebrows indicated nothing about the mind. The boy's head was small and his neck was long. His tight hair cropped close.

"He suck. Ol' bitch," answered his counterpart, a thick muscular Latino boy. Shorter and more powerful, he was fierce looking. His words rose urgently from his diaphragm and were given little shaping by his tongue—yet this lack of lingual sculpting created the improbable effect of haughtiness, made of raw force coupled with disdain. He had thick hard arms and big powerful hands, even with his stubbed fingers. A grown cat could sit on his palm. From his ear to his lip, he had a raised scar that glowed white on his face like a line of cocaine. Gallin's glance registered four piercings in his pockmarked face, three rings in his lip and one through his nose. "He a turtle. Slow bitch an ol' fucking turtle. Air. Air Shit. Air cock. Air cock fuck."

As if to demonstrate his subject's vulnerablilty, the boy took a box cutter from his pocket and stabbed a slit down through the

23

shoebox on the counter in front of him, through the groin of the red-on-black silhouette of Michael Jordan flying. Alarmed, Gallin pretended not to see the stab; he heard himself whistling and immediately stopped. That night, Michael Jordan was returning with his new team, the Washington Wizards—nee Bullets, but that name discomfited the nation's murder capital—to face his former team, the Bulls, in his old Chicago home. Gallin had seen the story on the Internet that morning. Jordan would pass by a giant statue of himself on the way in, his youth frozen in time, the basketball player as painted on an urn. The argument between the boys was about whether Jordan still *had it.*

"You don't know game bitch. Short bitch. No nigga in ya. Game sneak up and eat ya ass 'fore you know it begin wit G." The skinny black kid egged on the powerful Latino, dynamic wielder of the box cutter. He surprised Gallin with his fearlessness and Gallin worried for him. He thought when he turned around again he might see the fearless kid bleeding.

"He still a turtle."

"Yeah, you know about it, fucker."

"I know *what* it about. It all about who git who first. Who-git-who. Who-git-who." Gallin thought the Latino was quoting a song, a rap, a rhyme; he sort of chanted this refrain of who-git-who. He flicked out the little triangular blade of the box cutter and smiled madly at it. Then he calmly slid it closed, put it in his back pocket and looked around. "Fuck off," he said. "Bitch bled in Chicago. Give you that. Got no blood left to bleed. Wizards? Fuck."

Gallin looked over again, and the two boys smashed their forearms together, smiling. It was a hard form of handshake, obviously practiced. Gallin was reminded of thick-necked, prematurely balding boys in college who used to greet each other with clubby, enthusiastic head butts—Dartmouth men, a supposed elite, acting savagely, like bulls. It was difficult for men to touch each other. They'd do anything to mask the need. Gallin, drawn now to this dialogue, this stupendously declarative speech, tried to make more sense of it. To find what was hidden in it. That was the beauty of all speech, the hidden parts. The boys' language was debased but

24

surprisingly not ruined. It was raw, stripped, but it seemed to work through its very kinship with privation: it had power, almost music.

Having smashed forearms, the boys then said at the same time: *Gain star.* And again: *Gain star.* Gallin liked the hard sparkle of that. The tough eloquence. He took it to be a street mantra of ambition.

From where she had moved, by a stack of boxed footballs, the third staffer, a big dark fleshy girl stuffed cruelly into her referee uniform, called over, "Gang-sta my whore's ass. You can stick it in me, hmmph, if you got any of it. Gang-sta. Stoo-pit."

So Gallin had misunderstood *gain star*—it was gang-sta—a term Gallin had read in the *Post*—but no matter. To Gallin, the unmistakable current of violence in their talk was a thrill. It mixed explosively with something already in him, sparked the tinder in his bones. He wanted that kind of dialect—something fucking useful. These kids let their poisons piss out of them constantly in their speech. Their shit, their grudge, their venom hissed out every time they opened their mouths or gestured. Gallin tried to calculate what he had lost in his life by doing the opposite, by his years of capitulation, of swallowing his disgust. Protocol, manners.

Suddenly he tasted the nasty mint of all the stamps he'd licked—his own tongue, again, servicing—to thank people for parties, for parties he'd wasted his time at, his precious time. The almost good wine, the soft cheese, the pitiful people gathered to dodge the verbal darts or steal the modern art of those with more wit or dough. Polite hustling, acceptable scheming. He regretted his laughter at unfunny things said by successful people. He hated how much time he'd spent with people who'd never been hungry. Who'd only ever slept on a hard cold floor as a lark—and just now it made his shoulder muscles twitch and the tendons in his neck tense up with self-disgust. He considered the rifling rhythm of the two-syllabled *bitch,* as they said it. As these boys said it. And all the ways they said it. Bit-Cha. Bee-yatch. The black kid yelled over to the girl, "Shut up, bit-cha. Dumb bitch. Ignorant b-yitch." Gallin heard him hurl the word repeatedly against his teeth till he'd said what he needed to say with it.

25

As Gallin approached, the Latino tugged his gold-stuffed earlobe, proffering it in a gesture of solicitude.

"May I help you with something, sir? I bet I can," he said cheerfully, as if he had been transported magically into a television commercial. The boy's tone, his very voice, had changed utterly. It was polite and—Gallin couldn't help think—mocking, and it threw Gallin out of his rickshaw of sociological revelations. The surgeon's surprise turned to admiration: he had great skill, this boy, this actor. The aggressiveness that had built in Gallin, as he tapped his own anger using their borrowed cadences, melted away like a drunk's inhibitions. He tried to hold on to it. But it fled. He felt lightheaded.

This much was clear: these boys would never talk their way to him. There were tribes all over. Not just far away, like all the idiots feared, sequestered in mountain caves and Persian palaces, but here, right here, covered up good and thick in all sorts of business. Everybody was in a tribe.

"I'm doing some walking, that's all," Gallin said to the Latino. "Simple stuff. After lunch. I'm looking for good shoes for it."

"You're in the right place," he replied. "Walking's easy."

Gallin got a closer look at the boy, Miguel by the nametag. He had large, light sawdust-colored eyes, very active, glossy as if varnished, lushly framed by long eyelashes that curled up like bedspring coils. The eyes dominated his face. They almost looked kind. Caught by them, Gallin hardly noticed the metal punctured through his nose and lips, or the cocaine-like scar. Then Miguel shot these eyes at the far wall, beyond the competing greens of Packer and Celtic jerseys, past some fluorescent purple jerseys the doctor didn't recognize, beyond a tower of Timberland boot boxes and the caged silo of synthetic footballs being stacked by the big girl who'd said she had a whore's ass.

We're breaking up, we're breaking up. Into Gallin's head came a desperate voice from an old television show he used to watch with Bernardo when he was a boy. It was Bernardo's favorite show—about a bionic man. The plaintive voice belonged to the star, an astronaut, about to crash to earth—he said it at the beginning of

26

every program: *we're breaking up, we're breaking up.* It had made Gallin think of Yeats: the centre cannot hold. No, it can't. He'd wanted to tell Bernardo this fact about the center, but the boy was too young.

"You want something simple," Miguel said breezily. Suddenly it struck Gallin what was familiar in the boy: the boy was loved by his mother. A rich maternal love was a circumstance that became manifest in all its receivers. You could see it in their eyes— a shimmer of hopefulness, a ring of remembering, discernible no matter how thick grew the cloaking cataract of experience and ache.

"I know what you want, something like this, but plain," Miguel said, holding up a fairly normal looking tennis shoe. "We have it. Old school. You want old school. I'll get it in the back."

You might, thought Gallin. You might just get it in the back. Gallin's mind flashed to a vivid picture of the boy with a box cutter lodged in his spine. Disturbed, he looked up at the long wall of shoes. He had an odd thought: of Andy Warhol's early days in New York when Warhol was as yet just a commercial artist drawing ladies shoes for newspaper ads. Before the whole city had kind of *gone Andy* and started actually to look like him. It seemed as if the people here at Foot Locker had found a batch of Warhol's secret sketches from those pre-fame, still pedestrian days and gone ahead and produced them. In fact, the whole place was a Warhol type: antiseptic, Crayola hues, brand names and bright lights. The fact that there were hundreds of them, exact replicas like silk screens, all over the country—Warhol would have loved that.

And the violence in these boys. That, too.

Gallin walked the length of the store with a purposeful gait. He stood up to his full height—six feet four inches—something that, as soon as he did it, he realized he hadn't done in months. Breathing in deeply, feeling and hearing his neck crack, Gallin pressed his shoulders back against an imaginary wall. He remembered his father's strong hands pushing his shoulders back, as he had done often when Gallin was a boy. "Stand up straight," he'd say. "Don't slouch. Carry yourself."

Gallin had always tried.

Now the buoyant rubber soles, the cushiony carpet, and the smell of unadulterated newness, leather like fresh paint, all plied his senses with the idea of starting off in another direction. Stick and move, he remembered from his four exhausting boxing lessons as a young man. Stick and move. Gallin had had trouble doing both. He favored moving. Yet both were necessary. Bitch. *Bee-Cha.* Beeyitch. That girl had said: *you can stick it in me, my whore ass.*

He paid in cash.

Feet decked out in dazzling white and his sole-worn loafers in a plastic shopping bag, he made for the door. Enlivened, jazzed, his fresh rubber on the sidewalk, Gallin glanced back through the glass wall-window of the store. As he did he saw Miguel, looking shadowy, sealed in a glass world Gallin just escaped, throw his box cutter at a Jordan poster taped against the wall. It was an expert throw: the slate grey fin somersaulted through the air like a weapon in a kung fu movie. It nailed Jordan, aloft and akimbo, in his famous wagging tongue. Caught in vigil, Gallin nodded his head once at the boy in a surprisingly calm gesture of impressed approval. Surprising because he was not calm, but frightened. Gallin floored his pedestrian pedal: he lowered his head and walked. He hoped to hit the groove, that high point of exertion where the brain was greased and thoughts were pure and noble and free. It was a short walk though, and he would have to push it.

He was ten blocks along when he cut the corner too close at 73rd Street. Moving at a freeing pace, arms pumping, shaking off the world, he was channeling that smooth grace of speed skaters rounding a bend when he saw the old man for only a fraction of a second—just a glimpse of snow-white hair—before the collision that knocked him to the ground.

Gallin had been swinging the bag with his loafers in it too, wildly, and he clocked the old man with that as well, as he was going down. As stunned as if he himself had been bowled over, Gallin reached down to help his victim.

THREE

Declining help, Dr. Lester Rhodes—Gallin's longtime friend and mentor—rose slowly, cagily, looking around as if to defend himself against the gang that had just attacked him. For a second, Gallin thought the old man might throw a willowy hook at him.

"What the—the hell—are you doing? We're still in—in civilization, aren't we? My god," Rhodes sputtered, catching his breath.

"I'm so very sorry. Lester, oh fuck."

"Richard," Rhodes said, regaining his composure. "Richard, my goodness, what in god's name are you doing, speeding around like this? Like a dervish? Is someone chasing you?"

On hearing his name, Gallin's shame doubled.

"I don't know. I'm so sorry—I didn't, I—" he stopped.

Instinctively Gallin slid his hand up to Rhodes's head, where the older man was staunching a trickle of blood. He coaxed Rhodes's hand away, taking over the pressure.

"Damn it, Lester. You're bleeding. Jesus." Gallin bubbled with self-disgust. "This is horrible." Gallin pulled his hand away to look but quickly put it back. There was not much flow, but enough to need stopping.

"Lester, my office is right here, two doors down. Well, you know that. Hell. Let's just clean this up."

Gallin considered that Lester's bleeding made him seem almost healthier—the only convincing evidence that his insides were still pumping. Otherwise, pale as he was, he could have been a ghost.

"Are you alright to walk it, Lester?"

"Yes, of course," said Rhodes. "You know, Cicely won't let me out anymore on my own if I come home all bloodied, Richard."

He kept his head bowed in deference to the bleeding, but he turned slightly toward Gallin and looked at him sidewise, mischievously. "So desperate for patients now that you're out ruining them yourself, finally? How long have I told you—we are gatherers, not hunters, we medicine men."

"Yes, I know, Lester. I've always remembered. I can't believe this. I'm terrifically sorry."

Replaying the collision in his mind, Gallin was startled by how easy Lester had been to knock down. He winced now at the shaky deliberation of his friend's steps. Was it only the tumble? Or was this how he always moved now? Rhodes's vision, too, was weak. He crept along. How long had it been? He must have seen Lester last year, Gallin thought. But he hadn't. At least surely for the big millennium change—certainly, for the year 2000. But no, not then, either. Gallin had gone to Rome with Andrea for that. It was supposed to be a jubilee. Now he scoured his messy mind and uncovered the horrific, specific duration of his neglect: it had been three years since he'd seen Lester Rhodes. How could that have been? But the truth was it might have been five years before that. The friendship—the active part, if not the sentiment—had faded. Still, Gallin was wracked with guilt. He experienced a sharp sense of lost time, like that of a freed inmate.

"I see you're trying to stay with it," Rhodes said, pointing to Gallin's new white shoes and swinging his arm to mimic Gallin's striding. "That's a good boy, Richard."

"Yes, well, it's new—the exercise," Gallin replied. "Been recommending it to patients for years. Trying it out for myself. Not bad—clears the head. You seem well, Lester."

"Oh, it's attrition now, my friend. I'm well on a day like today, I am. Still have plans, of course—things to tend to, to get done. A promise I made myself, to keep plans. Might say though they're not as rigorous as before."

They traveled the half-block in a slow shuffle, ungainly dancers, failing the waltz.

"I don't believe it, Lester," Gallin started in cheerfully. He wanted to lead. "Have you been—"

30

"I'm far better off on the days when no one tackles me, I can assure you." He laughed softly.

"God, I'm sorry, Lester. I was thinking about everyth—"

"Don't think about it. I'm fine, just a bump. Anyway, as I was saying, you might just be the one if you keep it up."

"Here we are. Let's just go inside and have a quick look. The one what?"

"The one who beats it all and actually gets *younger*, Richard." Rhodes smiled, but as he stepped up it gave way to a grimace.

Gallin got his old friend up to the second floor in the elevator and onto the examination table. He missed Lester Rhodes. Why had he not thought of him? What if he hadn't run into him? How long would he have gone without remembering?

During Gallin's residency, Lester Rhodes had been about the most distinguished man in any room. Handsome, genial, respected; a scholar, a scientist, a surgeon of surpassing skill; he was, to boot, insouciantly wealthy. A friend and physician to the Rockefellers—he'd removed a (poorly kept secret) lesion from then Vice President Nelson—he was a collector of friends, books, anecdotes, arabesques, horses and wisdom. Rhodes had taken a liking to Gallin when the latter first arrived at Columbia Presbyterian, back again in his hometown of New York, hot and ambitious after medical school at San Francisco. With some of the other staff Gallin had wasted no time gaining a reputation for self-importance, or, in those more apt to be kind, hard-headedness. But Rhodes had stood firmly in the young man's corner, lending his stature and thus legitimacy to Gallin's evangelistic fervor about plastic surgery. In fact it was Rhodes's surprising—even countercultural—approval that had permitted young Richard to ultimately choose for concentration the field, thought then, even more than now, to be a featherweight path, superfluous and shallow.

"I don't see how they can argue that the inside is vastly more important than the outside, Richard," he had said then, referring to the body. Gallin remembered it vividly, taking down notes in Rhodes's cramped hospital office, practicing a doctor's scrawl.

31

"The evidence would seem to be in. Darwin's work is your ace in the hole. I'd say that Elizabeth Taylor, for example, is among the *fittest*, if you will, in evolution speak," he said. "If you could give to others a touch of what she has, physically, externally, wouldn't they be better suited for the world? Wouldn't they be more likely to thrive and prosper? To live longer and happier lives? That will be your study, and you will discover the answers. Health is many things. We haven't, honestly, begun to touch on it. It derives from everywhere."

The theory that beauty contributed to physical prosperity was exactly Gallin's argument, though it was not widely subscribed to. But as Rhodes pointed out, the evidence was everywhere, from the narcissistic peacock to Queen Cleopatra herself. The fact was: no one could tell you whether an attractive nose was a lesser contributor to overall health than a robust white blood cell count. There was no proof that didn't leave some other piece of evidence on the floor.

Socially too, Rhodes had guided him, taking him up to Woodbrook, introducing him around. That was in the beginning of the seventies. Woodbrook was a different world then—it was truly the country, with farms that were farmed and where the artisans outnumbered the courtesans. Not anymore. But it was a different world everywhere now: that was half Gallin's life ago.

Gallin bought the Woodbrook house in the summer of '73. They had spent summer weekends there that year in a rental, looking for a place he could afford, trying to manage a life that had become bewildering to him. Bernardo had just turned two and Christa, his wife, was getting sicker. The diagnosis was plasmablastic multiple myeloma. Blood cancer. A malignant stream: cancer in the very rivers of the body, in the fluid that traveled everywhere. It would eventually eat holes in her bones. By July, Gallin was leaking hope from wherever he'd managed to stash some. It was a horrible time: the country woke each morning on a bed of nails, prick and poison of corruption trickling down from the very top. We mourned our supposed innocence. You could taste the malaise in the water. Reporters sometimes described it as a cancer. But in the midst of it Gallin found a house so perfect it felt as if it had always been his. And the idea of a *home*, as it has since the ancients, buoyed the man. Two capacious stories of cool stone a half mile back from the twisting Seven Sisters Road, the house, with its great back patio ringed in ivy, was an oasis in a stand of cedar and oak. He bought it immediately, without being able to afford it. And the perfumed hope that came with new beginnings aroused his spirits, told him to believe the world was better than it showed.

But that July steamed like a kettle chamber. To escape the heat, Gallin and Rhodes spent a few days one memorable week on barstools in the arctic afternoon darkness of the Tavern Lavern watching the Watergate hearings on TV. They were awestruck as liar after liar appeared on the screen, raising their right hands and desecrating a nation. Gallin remembered now the comfort Rhodes had given him at the time, when the world—both his own and the larger one—was collapsing. It was nothing overt but ambient, like a piano played during dinner. It was simply the presence of something—or in this case, someone—honorable when things were breaking up all over. The comfort was so strong that Gallin thought—he hoped against his knowing—that the house he found would save his wife, his family. That it would be a kind of Magic Mountain. When he thought of that summer now, it came to him in a putrid light, jaundiced, humid, saturated like an old bandage. All except for the time he spent with Rhodes. That had seemed clean.

Gallin sealed the cut on Rhodes's head with skin-glue. It was nothing, thank god. Heads just bled. The brain loved blood. There was a time in your life, he thought, when you hardly knew any dead people. Then you learned history and their names came tumbling down like an avalanche trying to bury you. Then you knew people personally who died—that was different—then they called to you. Then you knew more dead than living, thought Gallin.

"Any pain?" Gallin asked.

"Feels quite good. The contact, I mean. Funny, it's a thing you miss that you don't anticipate. Everyone thinks they'll miss the soft touching—the hand-holding, lovemaking. But it's not that," he said. "It's much worse that you never bump into anyone after a while. First you're steered clear of contact, like you're an eggshell. Then, honestly, you get afraid of it and you steer yourself clear. Maybe it's practice for the final withdrawal," he said. "But no, nothing, to answer your question. No pain. Nothing *new*, that is." He smiled.

Just then, Gallin felt remorse that his career hadn't actually made a penetrating study of those issues Rhodes had so eloquently laid out for him thirty years earlier. His career had been less than that, and the answers it was his destiny to seek remained at large, unapprehended. Still it was something, what he'd made, right? He'd performed 11,000 surgeries, though what he learned he couldn't qualify. But hadn't his life exceeded his expectations, nonetheless? Who can imagine, after all, at thirty, all he will know of the world at sixty? Who could dream it? What Rhodes must know by now!

Yet great achievement, the Promethean kind that Rhodes had predicted for Gallin was rare—extremely rare. Suddenly, Gallin realized Rhodes hadn't had it either: missing from his time on stage was that critical penetrating act which posterity demanded. Lester had never really broken it open. For all his accomplishments he never tore an idea apart and found its seed, its block, its founding atom. He never stole that seminal drop from the clouds and gave it to us all plattered like the head of John the Baptist—saying, here is something newly consummated, synthesized, realized. Dance in celebration, Salome. He hadn't done the thing it took: cured something, discovered something, changed something. With all that intelligence, all the honors, the books and papers, what had he made?

Trying to walk a mile in Rhodes's shoes, Gallin remembered Will Rhodes, his and Cicely's only child, an uncontrollable schizophrenic, born late in the childbearing moment when Cicely was forty and Lester into his fifties. Schizophrenia was a brutal, vertiginous torture: it pulled the brain apart the way horses quartered a man. Young Will was a giant powerful boy—a bitter physical gift for a creature who so lacked self-control; and one summer afternoon when he was eleven he became deranged after striking out in backyard batting practice and beat Lester nearly to death with a baseball bat, shattering almost all of his ribs, trying, it seemed, to smash his heart. Mysteriously he took no swings at his father's head. A middle-aged man now, a doped-up docile bear declawed but caged, Will still lived, as far as Gallin knew, in the asylum in Connecticut where he was sent that week twenty-five years ago. Rhodes had never discussed the incident in any detail, and Gallin never asked about it. But Gallin knew from looking into Lester's eyes and from his own experience, too, that certain things were never overcome, but only lived beside in life. Being beaten unconscious by one's own sick, beloved son was surely one of them.

But everyone had their burdens, their turmoil, and Gallin, feeling a grotesque chagrin and driven by a grim mordancy he resented in himself, again took unsentimental measure of the man seated on his table. He pondered again whether there was greatness in Lester.

Had he achieved anything, in the end? Such judgment couldn't be helped: it was the human thing to do. Measuring was the survivor's prerogative. Salesmen, lawyers, athletes, burglars, politicians, dancers, doctors, obituary writers: judges all, and revisionists. The real criterion for evaluation was simple: Was that a life I would have taken? Would I trade?

"Will I make it, Richard?"

"This time, Lester. This time. But be careful—it's dangerous out there, you know."

Gallin jested, but in truth he'd half-forgotten that *he* had run over Rhodes, that *he* was the danger. He spoke as if Rhodes's own carelessness had finally caught up with him.

"I'll stay out of the paths of madmen then," he said. "Is that what you recommend?"

"If only one could, Lester."

"True, indeed. But we've got our good men, too."

"I'm always less sure of it."

"We do. You know, I thought I saw Bernardo today, over on Fifth," the old man said. "By the museum."

Gallin's hands froze. He looked at the floor, which needed sweeping. Human hair was always leaping from its body to the floor, escaping. He must remember to tell Janine to have it cleaned.

Gallin took his penlight and, holding Lester's chin, swept it so it danced across the old man's face. His cheeks, robbed of elasticity, had collapsed into a series of riverine canyons, withered tear tracks. Under his eyes, sagging crescents, heavy and yellow-grey, hung like spent tea bags. His face was pollocked all over by mauve-brown blotches, their scattershot shapes like bird droppings. His white eyebrows, once capable of silencing men by merely rising, grew wild as weeds in the middle, but had thinned on the wings to a few lonesome strands that jutted out spryly in odd directions. When he tried to focus on the light he looked furious and confounded, his cataracts giving back a ghost world.

He would die soon. They both knew it—and it made the affection long ago seeded grow up almost anew between them. An emotion long tethered by worldly concerns, now at the end of the road became primary and buoyant and free, beautiful as a cut gardenia bobbing on the water. It floated there between them, music of a deeper world, and they each acknowledged it privately and did exactly all they could with such emotion: nothing. No doubt Dr. Lester Rhodes's obituary was already in the queue at the *Times*, put to bed long before he would be, a few insignificant sentences to be filled in at the moment of his passing—the specifics: what time, where, and the official cause that was always so meaningless really. Gallin hated that it was written. Practical men were vultures, making their preparations, getting things done in advance. They call the living the quick for a reason. Gallin was overwhelmed by the desire to grab his friend and hold him. To say thank you. To say goodbye.

He looked again into the decrepit face in front of him, shining his penlight into the spoilt eyes—eyes half-starved for the clean line of sure shape, half-resigned to impressionism. Gallin heard the quiet rheumatism cooking in this husk of ruin, his friend, this prince of a man. He had let go more than thirty pounds: he was bean-poling, actually disappearing. It happened. Gallin could only imagine his friend's diet now, toast, tea—this strong, elegant man who used to drop his decorum only to devour his meals like a lion.

"You couldn't have," Gallin said. "You couldn't have seen him. He was killed, Lester. He was on the 87th floor."

"Good god. Good god, I'm sorry. I thought for sure, he, well, it couldn't—"

"It couldn't have been him, no."

"I'm so sorry, Richard. The family?"

Bernardo's death coming into the room made Rhodes's death suddenly less imminent. We can give death only so much space.

"The family is okay, considering. The young son, you know, almost one."

Gallin looked down at his new athletic shoes. They were out of place in the exam room.

"They received tremendous support—money, everything possible really. They even found his wedding ring and gave it to her. Incredible. They said he must have thrown it. Some kind of perfect moment they think he had. That's how we've chosen to imagine it, anyway. They didn't find the body. No expectation they would after about two weeks. Really a mess down there. It's a crater, it's a death camp. It's like hell."

"Good god." Rhodes stood. He was still nearly as tall as his protégé—skinny but he hadn't shrunk much.

"How about you, Richard? How are you?" He put a hand on Gallin's shoulder. Gallin bowed his head and shook it slowly. He drew some circles on the floor with his penlight. He flicked it off. He had no answer to the question. He didn't look up.

FOUR

When Janine rang him at five-thirty, fatigue sharpened the point in her voice as she announced that she was ready to go home—"It's Friday, Dr. Gallin." She also announced that there was a man there to see him. A friend of Peter's, he said. Gallin asked—he thought reasonably—what the man wanted. But Janine was by this hour working on the inverse—getting short as the week got long—and this never-ending Friday, with its morning maniac calling in threats, its noontime battery of Rhodes, and an unexpected late-day drama authored by a pampered augmentation princess who fussed and worried her peroxide-ravaged head, pre-surgery, like she was going on a trip to the moon rather than simply up a cup size, it was too much. Janine was dog-tired. She answered only—and with a little heat this time—that *the guy just says Peter said you would see him if he came by*.

Gallin persisted: "Is he a patient? Does he want surgery?"

"He could use a rhino," she said in a professional whisper. "But that's a guess. He's in a suit."

Gallin sighed.

"Okay, that's fine then, bring him up and have a nice weekend."

"I'll bring him up, Dr. Gallin."

Gallin jiggled the ice in his glass and polished off the two fingers of scotch he liked at the close of a business day. A sullen drink, the single malt. The burn from the berns, his old artist pal Sudol used to call it, back when they used to drink together. Gallin saw recently that Sudol had a big show up on Fifth Avenue at the National Design Museum. He'd admired the banner, a silvery sail with "Sudol in Glass" written in white sans serif, billowing in the breeze. The sign matched the winter sky, indicating, like glass,

38

what it was near. It was a clever banner, in sympathy with its subject. He should try to catch the show, he thought, catch up.

What next? Oh, right, Peter's friend. Last year Gallin had fired Peter Gunsenhauser, his nurse of eight years, after Peter voluntarily revealed that he was HIV positive. He didn't feel he had a choice. There was always a chance of infection in any operating room; while a body was open, everybody in the theatre was a part of a single organism. Fingers dug into chests, blades sliced away at eyelids, lips got filled through the gums with fat purloined from buttocks. Latex, the slim armor in this corporeal war, was merely a rubbery thumb in the brittle biological dike. Gloves, like condoms, broke.

Peter was a good nurse, with a gift for anticipating a need in the O.R. while otherwise remaining in the background, setting up the stages. It was a grace too little appreciated, Gallin now considered. In his mid-forties, Peter was soft-middled and thick-fingered, a gentle soul with a long head, a horseshoe jaw, and quiet blue eyes set close together, generously lidded. His jowls drooped endearingly. The large soft hollows of his temples beat assiduously, like pale hearts, as he worked and ground his teeth in concentration. His broad knuckles were covered in black hair, starkly for such a fair man, and he wore a beefy brown-blond mustache with thinning straight hair he parted sadly in the middle. He'd been an agreeable presence. Twenty years into his freedom flight from the center of America, vouchsafed to the West Village by way of Ohio State University and a dream, Peter was a buggering buckeye (Gallin liked the phrase) who'd fashioned a life, like so many other refugees, in the bustle and sprawl of Manhattan, ironically singling himself out at home for joining the masses here. He spoke flatly from the upper region of his nose, a vocal style that increased the likelihood of eye contact. Gallin supposed that Peter had cultivated this style to draw attention to his soft sky blues—a Darwinian wile, wonderfully subtle. A listener's eyes do seek a voice, invisible though it is.

Sad-eyed, blue-eyed Peter understood his dismissal was unavoidable after he admitted having the virus and, staring at the fact, he resigned as Gallin's nurse, though it was clear he'd held out hope for a better solution. After all, he'd volunteered the news. Couldn't something be worked out? But Gallin saw no other way.

Waiting for Janine to bring up Peter's friend, Gallin's mind wandered further. He could have been in Peter's place, he knew. Though he did his best not to think about it, he too had practiced a risky sexual game, if a different one.

Years before, just after having lost Christa and feeling therefore excused somehow, he went about town almost every night hell-bent, mainlining pleasure, determined to stave off the bitterness of his wife's blood tragedy through whatever means possible. That meant women—not quite as many as he could manage, but not far from it either. And it meant enough of the occasional, social drugs to keep his pursuits always fresh and his responsibilities at bay. It was a binge that resulted in a frantic, haunted man who saw a lot of sunrises from the wrong side of sleep. But that Gallin, the double-flamed despair burner, the hedonist, was a stranger now. He'd replaced that roaming, at-risk life with a series of unhappy monogamies, Andrea just the latest.

"Doctor Gallin, this is Mr. Edwards," Janine announced and backpedaled through the office doorway.

"Hello, Doctor," said the man stepping into the room. He looked back to be sure his escort was gone. He pushed the door closed behind him.

"Adams, actually. Nick," he said, smiling broadly at Gallin. They were alone in the house.

Rangy without being tall, long-armed and low-waisted, Adams's presence was kinetic. His white neck was as slender as a woman's, yet his glands bulged out of it like triceps. He presented an aura of contained ferocity. But the characteristic that pierced Gallin was not his confronter's sinew but his red hair, held down and darkened by thick gel. Gallin suspected it was about to burst free at any moment and reassert its demon charge: all its wiry insolence and clown fervor. Gallin loathed redheaded men; they triggered in him, in fact, a sort of phobic disgust. He recognized this as irrational—any pure generalization worked against high reason, wasn't that right?—yet he could rationalize it neverthe-less with insouciance. There was something dishonest about the redheaded male. The residue of childhood ostracizing, probably. The abuse and mental torture which only children can devise and which redheads universally attracted, cursed their characters, Gallin believed. He saw them as reprobates, unprincipled aggres-sors. Reckless. A social compact demanded faith—and Gallin intu-ited a damning faithlessness in the species of the flame-haired male. In fact, he had been beaten up by one in the sixth grade and never got over it. They were yet another tribe—a tribe in which the king and the jester would look the same.

Adams, who might have been either, stepped forward and offered his hand for shaking. He had given this moment serious consideration and thought that a handshake would be perfect. For his present role, that of blackmailer, edgy madman, goon, Adams had trained at the great University of America called The Movies. Adams favored the outside-the-law loner type as seen in Film Study 101, complete with stylized grit and knowing irony. Those boys just clobbered him over the head with cool. He liked best of all the Roman Polanski character in *Chinatown*—in that scene where he rips off Jack's nose. Adams believed he had his own genius just like that, but that the world was too immature to see it. If he could only put his pain on screen or on stage, he thought, the world would never look away. But that was another topic.

Gallin didn't reach for Adams's offered hand. He simply stared at the man, feeling both repulsed and stupid for leaving himself so vulnerable. There was a dimension to this lament that went beyond his present predicament to his overall weakness, his recent helplessness.

Adams looked down bemused at his own extended hand, shook his head and withdrew it. Okay then, you don't want to shake my hand, fine, he seemed to say aloud, though he said nothing. He was gleeful.

"What do you want?" Gallin asked.

"I want to read my article to you," he replied, taking a seat across the desk. He wore a bright orange tie that to Gallin's mind burnished his redheaded agenda.

41

"You're going to have to leave. If you have any kind of problem with me," he said, "you can talk with my lawyers."

"No, but I think that you will want to hear my article. You're the star!" he replied.

"Why didn't you just read it to me over the phone then?"

Gallin remembered back to those first strange calls from Adams. Now he feared he had miscategorized him. Gallin had grouped him with the general plastic surgery malcontents he considered bitter but harmless. There was a difference between such people and the truly dangerous. If you didn't know it before, you knew it now—September 11 had made a new world order. Gallin's malcontents were mostly dissatisfied with themselves. The truly dangerous hated others. They weren't projecting. They flew jetliners into buildings. Whereas the nut jobs, the losers, the kooks, the freaks, the mutants that plastic surgery sometimes attracted, they were different. They weren't dangerous, except perhaps to themselves. When Adams had started calling, Gallin pegged him as part of the softer group, like a spooked dog growling at ghosts, mad about something he couldn't fight. Gallin had listened because he thought Adams was harmless. He figured the episode, like so much else, would fade away. Besides, Gallin was frayed on the inside himself and it was a perverse comfort to hear this stranger berate him in these strange phone calls, incriminate him solely for the crime of being who he was.

"I've been investigating you," he would say, "you are a reprehensible man. You have no respect for human beings. Other people mean nothing to you."

It was blanket censure laid out on the line, and it dripped into Gallin's perforated heart. He listened to it silently more than once. There was never a specific accusation. And so, really, how could he argue? We were all guilty. Gallin not least—and now he had outlived his wife and his only son. Guilty. The masochist in him wanted the calls. He took them like a beating. He hoped they purged.

"I didn't read it over the phone because it wasn't finished yet. Besides, I wanted your full attention," Adams answered. He paused and then he said, "Why didn't you ever say anything back to me on the phone? I mean, when I called you and told you I'd get you?"

Gallin thought about this.

"Because you sounded like a child."

"Really."

Gallin emptied some ice into his mouth and chomped down on it.

"I'd offer you a drink, but I have a rule against drinking with extortionists," he said.

"I doubt that."

"You doubt what?"

"I'd say you probably have most of your drinks with extortionists. Legal ones. The protected. Lawyers, businessmen, producers. Do you know any producers, Dr. Gallin?"

Adams smiled the whole time he spoke, which was hard to do. He often practiced it. His teeth were extremely white and straight and false looking, especially being so egregiously exposed. They were also slightly too large, as if he'd got them on sale. And the poor piece of flesh that was his nose was braided like a cruller. No doubt it had been pulverized successively and it appeared that the last blow, which had been a right cross, had even knocked his freckles all to one side. Gallin was overwhelmed by the desire to fix this nose. Could he make this all disappear if he could get his hands on that sad atrocity? For Gallin it was not uncommon to change a life with his skill. Yes, he wanted to hammer away at it, start scraping down the mangled bone with his chisel. No procedure was as deeply satisfying as the rhinoplasty—reconstructing a person where he breathed. You could almost make a man honest if you straightened his nose correctly.

Adams crossed his right ankle over his knee and leaned back, exaggerating his ease. "I assume you don't know any producers then," he said.

"Am I in danger right now?" Gallin asked, point blank. He would have liked another scotch.

The question took Adams, who until then had been moving according to his script, by surprise. It was direct, too straightforward. He uncrossed his legs and leaned forward. He caressed the attaché on his lap.

"Doctor, as a young man I was a Golden Gloves boxing champion. If you are a champion, you learn how to fight, and when. That's all I'll say."

"But you didn't say anything."

"This is not the time to fight is what I said."

"No, you didn't."

"It's what I meant."

"You have something to propose then? I'm thinking to propose that the police come over here."

"I was let in. I didn't break in. Besides, you don't want the police. You're an educated man. Look at all these books. All I want to do is read to you. That's all. That's a pleasure for a man like you, right? Get your opinion?"

"I'm being picked up in fifteen minutes."

"Or maybe were you planning to leave in about—" Adams looked at his watch "—a half hour or so and go to your garage and get your Mercedes and drive to Woodbrook? So you can have drinks with extortionists? That could be your plan too, I think."

Gallin felt violated and angry with himself. He was an easy mark.

"But it doesn't matter about your plan," Adams continued. "Fifteen minutes will probably do. Can we get started though? You'll only want to hear the beginning anyway, is my guess."

Adams produced his ten-page manifesto and began quickly to read:

"It's called *Dying for Plastic Surgery*. I think it's catchy, the title. Here goes. 'Dr. Richard Gallin probably has AIDS. He doesn't know if he does or not. This fact will not stop him from performing plastic surgery this week in his richly appointed townhouse near Park Avenue. Nor will it stop him next week either, for the startling fact of his probable infection has not stopped him yet from operating on the innocent. He is unmarried and for nearly twenty years lived a high-risk lifestyle. Yet he has never been tested for the virus. The reason for Dr. Gallin's irresponsible reluctance is simple: he is afraid to know. He prefers ignorance. Given his history, so would you—'"

44

"What the fuck are you talking about? Get the fuck out of here!" raged Gallin, standing up. "What kind of trash is that?"

Adams was calm, not moving.

"Why did you fire Peter?"

"What are you talking about? Peter Gunsenhauser? What's Peter got to do with this? You obviously know why I fired him. Why is Peter talking to you? That's a better question. Peter knows the situation. What you're saying is ridiculous."

"Why should Peter be tested and not you?"

"Nothing requires me to be tested. I'm not at risk. I don't need to explain this to you. Who the fuck are you?"

"I'm Peter's partner. That's why he's talking to me. What you do to him basically you do to me."

His partner—his lover. Oh Jesus, Gallin thought, now it's a redheaded boxing faggot I've got on my hands. This gave Gallin trouble. He liked to categorize and Adams wasn't fitting in anywhere. Gallin drew all his impressions of gay culture from the stray men—hardly a representational segment, to be sure—who brought their waxed chests and tough guy-prissy sensibilities up to his office, wanting desperately and more honestly to transform themselves than any people he had ever known. If they had to start with something physical so be it: take my hips, I am a snake inside; lift my cheeks, I am an angel singing; raze my scar, I am pure and shall begin again. Whatever it was. They were brave that way, he thought.

During his debauched days Gallin saw more sorts of people more often and judged less. Back then, it had seemed strangely romantic: all the tragic composers, designers, and dancers of marvelous promise hogging all the obituary ink. These days he even sensed in gays a perverse streak of disappointment that their lives were no longer killing them, that real soldiers had replaced them in real trenches in the news, and that they were no longer practically guaranteed, indeed scheduled, to be dying for their art, which was, of course, themselves. A cause, a tribe, a movement needed tragedy. There is nothing so frivolous, sometimes, as staying alive.

45

That was something they had in common. Gallin had felt the same way. Twice now he'd felt that stupendous pain that comes with the unreasonableness, the senselessness, of living on. First when Christa died, and now Bernardo.

"You're going to need to get out of here right now," Gallin told Adams.

The sensation of loss this time, with Bernardo, was lonelier and quieter, but it weighed the same.

"My deadline is in two weeks," Adams said. "You want to talk before that—I'm available. You can reach me at Peter's—you still have the number I assume," Adams said snidely.

Deadline, thought Gallin. You don't have a right to use that word.

"I've got nothing to say to you. No one would publish your drivel."

"I'll just leave you a copy then." He threw the stapled sheets onto Gallin's desk; they landed on the new mask. "Thank you for your time. I'll let myself out."

It was true Gallin had never been tested. It was true that he feared a test. But he could hardly be unique in that, and it had been a long time since his behavior warranted a worry. Still, any accusation in the media, however toothless, could be as powerful as a conviction. An accusation raised doubt, and doubt in his business was a killer. Patients needed faith. Was he right to think Adams had merely drivel? Was it so ridiculous, this accusation? One of the women Gallin had an affair with had a husband, a producer, who died of AIDS. She'd always claimed the marriage was nothing, a ruse and she a beard, but had it ever been consummated, he wondered? The man had been handsome and not effeminate. There was another twentysomething girl he used to have sex with regularly. She'd never quite learned to take care of herself and left the city abruptly, rumored to have been infected. But there were always rumors like that in those days. There were more women too, of course. But he would know something by now, wouldn't he? Some symptom would emerge if he were a carrier. Yes, there was a possibility, but he was sure there was nothing to it. He was healthy. What he couldn't afford to become was the poster boy for the requisite testing of doctors. He didn't even think it a bad idea, but he couldn't be the one. You couldn't be associated with HIV in any way and expect people to keep showing up for surgery. They wouldn't. This Adams may have had nothing, but it could be a big dangerous nothing if he handled it wrong.

Gallin watched from the window as outside Adams bounced down 73rd Street on his toes, shadowboxing as he went, catching with soft right hooks his attaché as it swung up in rhythm with his step. He had a pretty rhythm. Gallin watched him through a web of leafless branches, watched him shrink into the distance.

He turned and walked the length of his office, a bounce in his own step. He wanted to put his walking shoes on. He poured himself a short scotch, without ice.

"Motherfucker," he said to a globe made in 1977. With a long finger he traced the great red expanse of the Soviet Union, climbing the Urals with his pinky. With his other hand he conjured a fist and shook it. "Fucking terrorist," he said.

FIVE

Shooting clays on Saturday morning calmed him: the rat-a-tat-tat of buckshot splattering against the low sky made a frenzy in the woods that matched the maelstrom in his mind. It mitigated, temporarily, his personal fever. Gallin imagined bringing the redheaded Adams out here and filling him full of shrapnel. When a crimson clay went up he muttered to himself "Dance," picturing a helpless Adams doing a terrified jig. Shooting, Gallin felt powerful, and rugged. Even as Fred regaled him with ribald stories, Gallin felt nobly alone.

But in the afternoon, freshly showered—the air of able rusticity scrubbed off him—he began to feel angry again, and anxious, as though he'd forgotten an important clue just revealed to him. Andrea had taken the dogs to the Thiessens, where she was assisting June Thiessen with some last minute party preparations. Alone in the house, Gallin tried to uncoil.

Uncharacteristically, he poured himself a scotch at two-thirty to take the edge off his mood. He turned on the Knick game and settled into a favorite armchair with the week's mail. A stock subscription offer caught his eye. The glossy brochure—with its photos of jubilant airbrushed model-mothers brandishing giant white teeth—described the brilliant future of a six-year-old medical devices company, an area Gallin had flirted with in the past. He held two patents himself, though neither had made it to market. The company he now read about claimed to have created a device to prevent ninety percent of all crib death. Brutal statistics and moving testimony from bereft parents was the sticky peanut butter in this wholesome sandwich of profitability, the jelly dolloped on by endorsing doctors who undoubtedly owned options

48

in the firm. Nothing new under the sun, Gallin thought. When he glanced up again, the Knicks were down by eighteen points. He poured himself a second scotch. Less than an hour later he was sipping his third when it occurred to him that crib death was perhaps the most horrible two-word phrase he had ever heard. The bland infant mortality was like a lullaby beside it.

When Andrea returned, she was cheerful and bright-cheeked as she bent down to kiss him. He felt the clean country cold escaping from her scarf and hair. His own head felt on fire.

"Who's winning?" she asked.

"Not even a game," he replied. "They dialed it in. No heart."

The basketball game had disintegrated steadily until it failed even to resemble a professional contest. The Knicks were down thirty-six. Garbage time players, millionaires all, stumbled around the court as though shod in the wooden clogs of the original Knickerbockers. They flailed pitifully as the acrobatic Kings of Sacramento soared over them, laughing, dunking, thumping their chests.

"You smell like my father," she said, waving her hand in front of her nose. Still, she smiled.

"What's that supposed to mean?"

"The alcohol," she answered. "That sweet alcoholy smell in the afternoon. My sister and I used to call it poisonberry. You know we have to leave by six—it's an early party."

Andrea left the room and Gallin followed her. She stood in the big coppery kitchen, chopping stem bottoms from a bouquet of sunflowers she'd brought in. He came up behind her and slipped his arms around her, fastening his hands together in front of her stomach. He let his hips sway from side to side, trying to move her along with him.

"God, how many did you have?" she asked.

"I had one," he said, a bit stridently. He stopped swaying, but left his hands clasped around her.

"Oh," she said, wriggling free.

Andrea put the large flowers in a blue-and-white ceramic vase and placed it on the windowsill above the sink. The petals filtered the late sun like church glass. Gallin felt a wave of affection for her for bringing them.

"Oh, they're beautiful," she said, stepping back to admire them.

"They are. They're like faces in the crowd," said Gallin.

"Hmm. Yeah, sort of."

She reached out and touched one of the flowers.

"Would you like a glass of wine?" he asked her.

"I'll wait," she said. She raised her wrist and looked at her watch, a superfluous gesture meant to bring Gallin's attention to the time. She could have as easily consulted the wall clock directly in front of her. "We should leave in an hour—an hour and ten minutes at the latest."

"Does that leave us time for a nap?" he asked suggestively. No way can she clam up again after that cruel business on Thursday night, he thought. Not up here.

"Oh, I don't think so." At her side, she shook her watch-bearing wrist. "No. But later, after, yes for sure." She drew a finger softly up the length of his thigh, a gesture she thought helpful with the brush off. "We've got to shower and get dressed and—"

"I'm fresh. I've showered."

Andrea picked up from the floor a knotty round of pale green stem that had skirted off the cutting surface. She held it up to her nose and then threw it away.

"How was the shooting?"

"It went well. It was fine. Invigorating. Fred's funny. He's like a bear out there. He couldn't hit a thing today, but I bet if he had to shoot his dinner to feed that gut of his he'd never miss."

"Ha," she said, pulling her sweater over her head. "He'll be at Donnie and June's tonight, won't he?"

"He said he would, yes."

She tossed the sweater on one of the kitchen chairs.

"Is he bringing that stripper?" she asked.

"Andrea, she's not a stripper," he replied, adding, "I don't know if she's up this weekend. He didn't say."

"I bet she is. She's always with him now."

50

"You know what he did tell me though? He was talking about his father dying. He died on New Year's Eve, 1999. So you know what Fred said to me? He laughs and says, 'like I told my brother, I guess the old man wasn't Y2K compliant.'" Gallin chuckled uneasily.

"That's awful."

He had followed her upstairs, telling her the story. Now he was watching her calibrate the shower temperature. She made incredibly minute adjustments to the chrome knobs, waving the back of her hand through the stream.

"But that's the way to deal with it. To deal with things like that, I think. To make it a joke," he said.

"That's one way, I guess. Damn, I can't get this temperature right," she said.

"Turn it off," Gallin said. "Start again."

"Richard," she said, "I'll get it. Thanks. Now I have to get ready, okay? You could bring me a glass of wine now. White? Please? Something that goes with the weather?"

Downstairs, he poured her a glass of Sancerre and left it upstairs on the console table outside the bathroom. Inside Andrea was singing, "Alouetta, gentille Alouetta. Alouetta, je te plumerai."

Gallin went back downstairs and poured another scotch. I'm just going to have a good simple time tonight, he said to himself. He caught a dark picture of himself reflected back by the glass door leading out to the terrace. He stopped and faced it. Outside, darkness had swiftly completed its evening assumption of command, but inside the warm cozy light reminded him of melted butter. It was nice, the man-made light. Gallin stood up tall to his reflection, pushing his shoulders back. He nodded at it gravely. "To a worry-free, to a simple eve," he said to the other version of himself. Let's have one for old time's sake—a regular good time. He raised his glass.

IF A community was like a computer, the Theissens' party was meant to reboot it. The holiday gatherings—those that weren't cancelled—had all been lugubrious, with people already having seen their friends recently enough at funerals or memorial services. September 11th was the elephant in every room. That year, the singing of "Auld Lang Syne" could almost paralyze. People wept not for a year dispelled but for an age.

Now, the New Year begun, people were testing out a tentative but powerful hope that the world would move forward. It could not resume, of course, but it might proceed. The horrible events had delivered a rebuke of sorts, it was generally conceded. People were conscious of taking the opportunity to be more grateful for what they had—inasmuch as they were capable of gratitude. But their dedication to renewed appreciation was profound. The party was to be a moment marking this dedication, not so much celebratory but participatory—the first step up the long ladder to the future. One needed to respect the dead, but to do it by going on living.

Gallin, however, was in a different place than the other somber but hopeful revelers. His world shook more. He was not ready. It couldn't be a regular good time because Gallin hadn't regained dominion over his demons—he couldn't halt their hectoring—and the booze, which he kept at steadily through the night, switching types but never ceasing, curtailed not his angst, but his respect for propriety. The early scotch was a poor prescription; he knew it almost as soon as he filled it. The first drink had too easily oiled his emotions and then the third had brought him nearly to tears over crib death. Soft little life, dumb and wanted, snuffed out like a candle. Gallin ached for the innocence.

At the Thiessens, he stood inches above the crowd and— armed with a singular depth of feeling—he felt that in his grief he could see truth in a way others couldn't. He perceived his advantage in height as emblematic of a more comprehensive superiority. But even with the toast to his reflection fresh in his mind, and the buoying dual satisfactions of his exceptional height and insight, the good time he'd planned eluded him.

Taking in the people, his friends, his extended circle, the red-faced, perfumed, tailored, control-hosed, frightened, shocked

52

and decadent, he felt the shameful *lostness* he remembered from looking at old class photos, when the questions—Who are these people? Did I really know them once?—brought answers that simply proved one's isolation. Proved it beyond a reasonable doubt. If the people you spent your days with were not enduringly important, as his faded classmates were not, and like these people must not be, then you were essentially always alone. Solitude, then, was the truth.

He began to insult people around seven o'clock. By eight Andrea was outraged, rolling her eyes at first and then lowering her head and exhaling demonstratively, finally stabbing him in the thigh with her knuckle. Conversational subjects ranged widely, yet no matter what was struck upon, Gallin lashed out with vituperative astonishment at his friends' collective ignorance.

"You have really such a small idea of what you're talking about it's a wonder you're bold enough to speak," he said to Andrew Patricof, a music executive who had just claimed that Afghanistan was "geopolitically the real sleeping giant of the second half of the century." Gallin walked away in disgust, after adding: "If you're going to issue such absurdities, you should at least put on your white makeup and your big red nose."

Patricof, at least, was just an acquaintance. In another group Gallin found his host, Donnie Thiessen, talking about anthrax. Thiessen, a handsome corporate lawyer celebrating his tenth year of marriage to a woman who had grown to look disturbingly like his first wife, spoke in an authoritative tone about this suddenly famous biological agent: "They've got it all over. It's incredibly dangerous and incredibly common. You can have a couple of cows and if you know what you're doing, bingo, you could devastate a city the size of Chicago."

Another one trafficking in fear, Gallin thought. He liked Donnie well enough, but he couldn't contain himself.

"Donnie does malice, is that it?" he asked. "First let me tell you that the Cipro—the wonder drug you've all been taking, the one I've prescribed for half of you—doesn't do a thing. It won't help you in the case of a weaponized anthrax attack, not one bit.

So don't feel insulated, don't feel all right about it. You won't be okay. That said, you might want to be a little more sober—don't go destroying Chicago so fast in some fantasy where you watch with your vaccinated eyes because you can afford the drug. You'll die too," Gallin was cool and matter-of-fact, glib. Donnie looked like he'd been slapped. "But you are lucky, Donnie, because you're mind-bogglingly wrong about the rest of what you said. It's not at all easy to make anthrax. Fred's got a couple of cows over at his place. Excuse me," Gallin spotted Fred fifteen feet away and yelled, "Fred, can Donnie here use your cows?"

Not knowing what in hell Gallin was talking about, Fred threw up a fat hand and shrugged his eyebrows and shoulders to say sure, why not?

Gallin continued to Donnie: "I'll tell you what, I'll arrange for you to spend a year with Fred's cows, and you see if you can do any damage to anybody but yourself."

"Jesus, Richard, I'm just saying that it's out there—it's available, that's all."

"Available to whom?"

Gallin, like a schoolmaster, let the word *whom* spread out and linger.

"To people who really want it."

Gallin put his arm around Fran Ford and pulled her close, laughing. Fran smelled like a rose garden. She was the tallest woman in the room, nearly six feet in her modest heels, a good-looking woman with short dark hair and a proud bearing. He was tempted to nuzzle her, give her elegant earlobe a playful little bite. "Well then, Fran here would like some if it's that easy, Donnie. Fran would use it to kill Harold, her uxorious husband. She'd kill him dead, I bet, in about a minute if there was a simple little powder that would do the trick." Gallin nodded over the top of the crowd to where Harold Ford was talking to a very young woman in the corner. "If it were that easy, I think more than a few of us would meet our ends abruptly."

"Jesus Christ, Richard," Donnie said.

"Look, unless it's Mrs. O'Leary's cow, Chicago has nothing bovine to fear. Trust me."

"I still believe it can be manufactured without too much trouble. I've read quite a lot on this."

But Gallin was off in pursuit of the waitress passing hors d'oeuvres. His mouth was dry; he was hungry.

"I'll tell you what—I feel sorry for Andrea," Donnie said, as Gallin trotted away.

"Oh, Donnie," Fran Ford replied, "he's just being miserable. It's his right. We should all be a little more publicly miserable."

For the party, scores of kerosene lanterns illuminated the capacious main room. They lined the walls along the floor and hung from the exposed wooden beams above like big gems on a flaming necklace. They flickered with a dubious message, suggesting a return to simpler times. For, in addition to a renewed appreciation for life, the nation's shaken citizenry—in fierce pain still, squinting through the blinding smoke of aftershock—was also feverishly pledging a return to simpler things, to what's really important, as the common parlance had it. And the lantern effect—with its primitiveness, its notion of warmth, its hearth echoes—was a precious effort by the Theissens in service of this pledged return, meant to produce a palliative comment on— and recognition of—the importance of the elemental in the world. It meant to say we might forsake our progress and still be who we are.

But that was a ridiculous proposition, arrogant, and Gallin, having just admired the electric light in his own house—it was absolutely no time for going backward, damn it—wasn't buying any retrograde spirit candy, licking flames or no. What had cocktails by lamplight to do with getting whole, really? Or with living and dying? Experts in the evocative now, scientists of our own symbolism and circus masters of our own emotional triggers, we hardly knew what was real, so adroitly did we fool ourselves. The real was too hard to trace through all the self-manipulation.

Into his mouth Gallin popped another lobster puff. Or so they were winningly called by the five-foot Latina fidgeting in coarse hosiery and a black maid's dress, cheap white lace collar looking like a doily. Her broad young face was covered in a thick manila paste meant to cover acne. She smiled up at him, holding a silver tray.

"Lobster puff?" she asked.

"Delicious!" he replied, smiling back.

They were flaky and hot, sweet meat in the middle. Must be French, he thought. My, the French could bake. There was a simplicity he might subscribe to. He wiped his fingers absently on his trousers, stuffing an unused napkin into his pocket with his clean hand.

Turning for the bar, Gallin noticed across the room a man wearing a tuxedo hunched over on one knee—a waiter who had dropped a tray. The scene bothered him. Why did everyone move away? Surely they saw him, hunched over like that. To his horror, Gallin concluded that he was the only person in the room capable of genuine compassion. He started toward the man to help, weaving his way around the other guests, elitist barbarians. The thought struck him: What he should do is take the Latina in her miserable costume and the kneeling, slippery-handed waiter and the three of them should hightail it out of here. He could buy them dinner down at one of the restaurants on the lake. Hell, he should take the whole staff. Gallin was now slithering like a housecat through the crowd, his heart slick with joy. A liberator! he thought. Richard Gallin, Bolivar! Richard Gallin, gang-sta savior. He celebrated himself. He would tell the kneeling waiter: Leave it there on the floor—go and get the others!

But with only a few feet between them, the waiter stood and whirled about in a single motion, stopping Gallin in his fervid tracks, in a spot from which he recognized immediately his mistake: the waiter was not a waiter at all but a violinist. He hadn't dropped any tray of food but was kneeling rather to extract his instrument from a beautiful red velvet-lined case. Now he held the glistening hourglass of wood and string out before him with immense dignity, as though it were a combination of scepter and newborn.

Gallin, crestfallen liberator, stepped back. But he remained captivated by the violinist who, having traveled in mere seconds the long improbable road from forlorn waiter to stately musician, had just transformed himself as decidedly, as magically, as a pupa. Gallin was upended by the change. He was filled with admiration, with a sense of witnessing the honorable. Then without introduction, without even a courteous quieting of the crowd, the man straightened as if at military attention and began to play Vivaldi—clear and fine, soaked in sadness.

Of all that humans dreamt up, music was the most mysterious for Gallin. A fair athlete, if late-bloomed, and a passable painter even, in his youth, and a scientist—a surgeon, after all—Gallin was an adept in the civilized world, urbane, experienced, knowledgeable and yet music had resisted him. It kept its secrets, and this cloaked essence had unusual power over him.

The booze was starting to suck his skin closer to his bones: it stirred again his shipwrecked dreams of liberation, while the music mixed in his lofty heartbreak. The flicker of the candles reminded him, despite himself (the motif had worked!), of a time earlier in his life when he'd believed he was the owner of a soul—a real tangible thing that would float up after him when all this withering was over: his ticket, a way he could live forever. If anything still spoke to that belief it was music. He listened now for clues. His mouth was dry, and his lips so badly chapped that he was peeling little translucent epidermal strips from them with his teeth. But his eyes were moist, fed by rivers in his mind that ran down from enchanted hills above the plains of reason. Music was the place Gallin always felt he should get to, but could not find. He clapped ferociously when the first piece ended, startling those next to him but forcing their hands, too, to applaud the player. The violinist gave a slight, embarrassed bow.

The applause slid slowly back up the guests' sleeves and the violinist charged into the last beatless smacks of it with the first notes of the next sonata. But Andrea's voice broke Gallin's spell. From the hallway behind him Gallin heard her say, "No, no.

Stop." She was giggling. A man's voice softly admonished her: "Quiet—quiet!"

Gallin took an instinctive step toward the voices only to stop, suddenly. He didn't recognize the male voice and he was glad. He didn't want to know it. He closed his eyes and let the music pull him back from confrontation. The violinist was deep on the heavy strings, spooking the room with a groaning larghetto. Gallin let the music overtake the voices, let it flush them away. Then it was as if he heard nothing at all. He didn't even bother to look for his coat before leaving, waving goodbye only to Fran Ford, who was waving hopefully to him from afar.

SIX

"These are excellent," Ana Garibaldi was saying over her shoulder, taking in the collection of tribal masks on the low table in front of her.

Gallin had made it home. Woke that morning after a brief comatose slumber, decided against examining the previous evening for shame, left Andrea an even-tempered note to say *enjoy the dogs for the week—Love, Richard* and fired his Mercedes coupe back toward the city. He ripped off eighty miles in fifty minutes, a record, his only company most of the way the bare gray roadside oaks and a convoy of eighteen-wheelers whose high backsides swayed in the wind like Marilyn Monroe's. He was flying, weaving playfully between the trucks, a part—for a few fine minutes—of their barreling corps. One thing you could say about the tragedy: truckers and doctors, lawyers and bricklayers, every disparate group that claimed citizenship—their respective rigs now uniformly adorned with American flag decals—had found common ground. It was good to know your enemy. It made things clear.

The Mercedes, which had last spring cost Gallin approximately eleven breast augmentations, punctured the wind like a missile. And the truckers, who on September 10th might have run him off the road for spite, instead hooted him on, blowing their big foggy horns at him like members of a marching band. Gallin and the German race car made good sport of chewing up the gravel for them, spitting, as it were, into the wind that rocked their trailers. His head ached but his heart roared.

Now he was home standing behind the leather sofa on the top floor of his townhouse, a man of wealth and taste, headache behind him, stabbing a chopstick into a steaming mug to accelerate the diffusion of tea. He pushed his chin to the side; his neck cracked quietly. The purge of last night's letting go, the adrenaline of the drive, this new woman in his living room. He might be free!

Gallin looked over at Ana Garibaldi, perched on the sofa with such loveliness as he could not describe. He strained anyway to try. Balletic poise, preternatural grace and, the clincher, gymnastic sangfroid, came to mind. But hitting upon the last, most homely phrase, which seemed more aptly to describe a bullfrog, he grew concerned that he was perhaps too eager in the assignation of beauty. He often jumped the gun, as it were. He knew it. He rarely tried to prevent it.

Yet, as she sat there, hovered really, in his house, and as Gallin, studying her, pinning a teabag hard against the bottom of the mug, bleeding it until the yellow-brown stain expanded in the water like a storm cloud, well, for the first time in recent memory Gallin could not believe the largesse of his luck. It was so, he was sure of it: Garibaldi was beautiful.

Throughout Gallin's life the company of beautiful women had trumped all. They expanded all possibility, made the world larger. There was a time, years back, when the overpowering effect of beauty on him had triggered an atypical bout of introspection. He wondered: was he a shallow man? But there was help from history: Helen's beauty had launched a thousand ships. And from poetry: beauty was truth. Indeed, beautiful women were natural in the world like sunrises, like mountains and oceans. They inspired. They changed perspectives.

Garibaldi leaned forward over the table to pick up another of the masks, and on the silky topographic island of her back Gallin became momentarily, happily, stranded. He glimpsed in relief her bra strap—surprisingly wide-banded, three hooks, demure—and through the white silk of her blouse he also noted soft Himalayan nubs of vertebrae that, like a trail of half-sunk pearls, scaled her spine in perfect measure before disappearing, like the past, into the tapered splendor of her long neck. Her dark hair was cropped short, made slick and luminous by some sort of gel; gold pyramids dangled on gossamer strands from her ears. Her skin was the ambiguous shade of tea. She looked like Nefertiti.

"Do you mind if we go through a couple of questions to help me orient the collection?" she asked. "I can do it straight—a line item method, if you will—but this way I think I can be more effective for you."

"Sure, ask away."

"My hope is—coming in with the little that I know about you and then, honestly, being very impressed with the pieces I'm looking at—the idea is to position your collection with a singular *raison d'etre*. Most of the—"

"Sounds good to me," Gallin interrupted. He handed her a steaming mug and walked around the sofa to sit beside her.

"Most of—or a very high percentage of the higher quality, small-to-medium size collections I'm asked to look at belong to psychiatrists, at least in New York. You have to understand that a collection's value can transcend the particular value of its individual pieces in certain circumstances. That's what I have in mind here. A collection's value can have so much to do with its organizing principle, with the collector's *raison*. The psychiatrists all mostly claim that their primary interest in the masks they collect is the unconscious motivations of the mask makers, the deep well of primitivism that modernity and affluence have done so much to bury. They talk a lot about Jungian archetypes, in transcendental worship methods, about the role of the mask in self-abandonment and the deliberate cloaking of the ego. And wish projection—you're wise not to get them started on wish projection." She smiled.

Listening intently, Gallin tried to determine what his own *raison d'etre* for collecting had been. Mostly he bought what he liked. Occasionally, though he was untrained in it, he speculated—buying what he thought might go up in value. His collection was split about even between what he'd acquired through dealers and pieces he'd found on his own travels. He was, of course, proudest of the latter. To be perfectly straight about it, he would rather have collected Ming horses and such, but for that you needed *real* money.

"The tea is delicious," she said. "Thank you."

"Not at all. Please go on. I am eager to hear how I can distinguish myself from these psychiatrists!" he said with a smile.

Garibaldi smiled again too. A layer of stiffening propriety, one he hadn't noticed until it vanished, dropped away from her like a spring jacket slipped off in the sun. She relaxed a little. He hoped she would strip away another layer. Reveal more.

"I don't mean to in any way disparage those collections, or any client I've worked for. Their *raisons* are legitimate and even powerful. But at the same time they are nearly impossible to convey—they won't leave the abstract in a package neat enough or intuitive enough to be expressed," she sighed, exasperated by this fact. "In other words," she took a deep breath, "No one gets it. It's too hard to communicate. The linkage between the pieces is too, well, recondite. People want to hear a story behind these things, about how they're related. How they came to be a collection. They want to understand. With the psychiatrists it's too obscure." She laughed a little as she said: "They don't call it the unconscious for no reason."

Gallin laughed and grazed her silk-sheathed shoulder as he did. "Okay, so what about these?"

There were eighteen masks on the low square table, with another half dozen on the floor beyond it, in front of the fireplace where a Duraflame blazed. There were another twenty downstairs in his office.

"It's an unorthodox approach," she began, "and if it doesn't fit we discard it right away, obviously."

"Fine—what's your plan?" Gallin asked conspiratorially.

"Wait," she licked her top lip, which had a strong pink 'v' at its center. The 'v' of a heroine, Gallin thought. "Actually, one more thing first. Why the appraisal now? Do you hope to sell?"

"Does that make a difference?"

"In some ways, yes. All valuation is subject to time. Like the stock market and anything else where money's involved." Garibaldi lifted her head and gesticulated with long fingers to indicate the handsome room and what it said about Gallin's

62

affluence. "You obviously know something about timing and valuation," she said.

"Some lucky guesses," Gallin replied, shrugging. But his modesty was false. His gains had been hard, hard work.

"But back to it, you intend to sell the collection?"

"I think I may."

"Okay, I'd like to ask why but I'll save that question. What I'd like to do now—sorry, how are you on time?"

"I don't have any plans—you have my complete attention."

"Okay, I'd like to advance a framework for positioning your collection. Then we'll evaluate the individual pieces within that framework."

"Sounds reasonable. Please go ahead."

"Here's where it's unorthodox. Normally, I'd ask about your purpose in putting together the collection, but in this case I'd like to suggest it instead."

"All right—"

"Since you are a plastic surgeon, it seems to me that gives us a special opportunity. In organizing any collection you get the chance, to a degree, to prioritize the importance of various considerations—aesthetics, historical relevance, cultural potency, etc. By bringing the collector's interest to the forefront of the value proposition, we can sometimes relegate the intrinsic worth of the individual pieces to second-tier status. In other words, the whole becomes greater than the parts. Do you follow me?"

"So far, yes."

"So if something's not as old, perhaps, as we'd like, we say the age doesn't matter—or at least not much—because that's not a prime motivating factor of the original collector. Age has little to do with why it fits into the collection."

"Right. Okay."

"Well, what I suggest is that because you are a plastic surgeon and your expertise is in beauty, we present your cardinal motivation as pure aesthetic pleasure. Nothing more. Throw out history and all the rest."

"But doesn't that devalue it? Some of these pieces are important. Your way I sound as though I wander through the world ignorant of culture, innocent of history. That I don't know anything but that it's pretty."

"No, no, Dr. Gallin. It's—"

"I've *been* to these countries. I've seen these cultures," he said. He didn't want to sound offended, but he was: she thought he was a shallow man. It was the thing he was always hiding. "This piece," he said, grabbing a marvelous-looking mask from the middle of the table. "I got this piece in Cameroon. It's by the Ekoi. I paid something like fifty American for it in '82 and it's been appraised at nine thousand."

"Dr. Gallin, please let me—"

Her eyes had lost their mirth, but were more intriguing for the loss. They were big almost yellow eyes. She put her hand on his knee.

"Richard," he replied, "Please call me Richard."

"Richard. What I meant is nearly the opposite of how you understood it. I'm sorry. I need to be clearer. What I suggest is that we present you as a unique collector in that you bring an uncompromised contemporary Western eye to your collecting. Not an eye ignorant of the past, but one containing an especially sophisticated knowledge of art, an inherently broad cultural literacy, and an expertise in what we'll call the human facial aesthetic. In other words, as Dr. Richard Gallin, your eye is uniquely able to remain unenslaved by the trappings of history and theory, and so will be free to recognize the art as it speaks for itself aesthetically, here today in 2002. You are uniquely able to get beyond the artifact and to the art, which is what makes these masks more than mere curios. By using your singular criteria, you can help the dignity of these inspired works of art escape from the *category* they're stuck in. You can liberate the art from ritual, from its anthropological cage."

Gallin loved it. He even wanted to believe it. And it was true enough: he couldn't tell you exactly how he chose his collection other than that he certainly had liked the pieces. That was a consistent factor. He'd found them aesthetically pleasing.

Garibaldi continued. "This is just an organizing principle I had in mind. But the collection I'm looking at now totally justifies it. And it could gain that unique position, I think, in the market that any collection seeks. Especially if you were going to donate it. Of course this idea pushes you, the collector, to the forefront, but I think it's the way to go."

Gallin held out his tea mug; they clinked their mugs together.

"If that's what you think, that's the way we go. Donation is something I'm interested in, but I hadn't considered seriously. If you think there's a chance that the collection wouldn't go directly to basement storage somewhere—"

"I think there's a very good chance it will be sought after."

"Really? Sought after? Who do you think would be interested?"

"I couldn't say for sure. The Walker maybe? I don't know yet."

"Really? Well—"

"Most likely only as a gift, of course."

"Hmmm."

"That's if we can really pull off this positioning and get away from the interesting but dead-horse ground that focuses on what the masks represent. We don't want anything in the catalogue that reads 'primal man is here showing his respect for the complex gods that animate him—' You know, 'in this case he believes his own face represents the gods insufficiently . . .'"

"Dear, don't knock that." Gallin's face grew bright. "That's what keeps me in business—all the people in New York who want their faces to more accurately reflect the gods' intentions!"

Ana laughed. Her teeth were straight and powerfully white. The wind blew noisily out on the terrace.

Gallin got up.

"Can I get you some more tea? Or something a little nicer? A brandy? It's a cold afternoon and I'm in need of one."

"That would be very nice," she said, getting up also and going over to the big window looking out on the terrace.

"So you'll write the catalogue or monograph or whatever it is? You'll organize the work?" he asked, pouring two cognacs.

"I'd love to," she said quietly, without turning toward him.

"You're expensive, I assume."

"Very," she answered. This time she turned and smiled.

"Okay then, we'll do it. You can start soon?"

"I could start the beginning of next month. But for our positioning effort I'm going to need a good deal of your time. I'll need to know more about you personally, to create the backstory."

"I'm all yours," he said. He walked over to her and handed her the snifter. "Would you like to sit?"

"No, no. I don't have windows like this. It'd be a shame not to look out."

Gallin stood next to her. They clinked glasses.

"You know," she started, "I need to say this. This isn't the first time we've met."

Gallin was heavy-hearted with the news. Things were going so happily and all was fresh and new, and now a link to the past.

"Yes," she continued. "It must have been twenty years ago—I give away too much by saying—but that's when it was. You gave a talk in the Art of Medicine series at someplace on Fifth, I don't remember exactly. I think it was the Met. Yes."

Suddenly, surprisingly, Gallin remembered: it was the week after Christa had died. That talk was something that, at the time, he believed he had to do—to go through with for the sake of his own continuity. Of course, in reality it wasn't something he'd had to do at all. It was nothing. Yet here it was, that decision, living on independent of him, choosing today to revisit him after decades, now with his son dead too. What lived and what died! A son dies and a meaningless talk lives on and on.

"You talked about preserving cultures in the face of such accelerated change. It was fascinating—on the one hand you spoke of the advances in medicine with awe, like a real evangelist. You could have practically been testifying before Congress for funding."

Gallin turned, staring at the orderly little fire. He could feel the pinch in his chest of those long-ago thoughts, passions. Ana went on.

"But on the other hand there was something in your voice where it seemed that if you could have stopped time right then, you would have. You said you were filled with sorrow because cultures were being obliterated by pure speed. Like a thought by an action, you said. I remember that phrase. And you said that we should remember that the jury was still out on whether a thought had ever been bettered by action on the thought's behalf."

"You remember it much better than I do. I'm flattered," Gallin said. "A little embarrassed as well."

"No, no. Don't be, not yet," she smiled at him. "We had a drink afterwards."

"Oh, god."

"No, it was fine, I'm just teasing. I practically made you do it. I had a friend with me, too—a girl I worked with, I can't even remember her name—but we got you to come to the Stanhope with us, to the bar."

"This I don't remember."

"You were very intense—quiet but polite. Nothing like you'd been on the dais—not talkative at all. You seemed so powerful to me. And so sad. I remember thinking—and this is how young and naïve I was—how could anybody so powerful be so sad?"

"That was a sad time."

"Do you think about it now, I mean, with all that's going on? Think about our speed and other cultures?"

"Not much, no. No answers for those things."

"Anyway, you said please excuse you. That night, I mean. You'd only had a sip of your drink. I thought you were going to the men's room, but you never came back."

"Oh, bad behavior. Terrible. I apologize, if you'll—"

"No, don't apologize. You paid the bill," she smiled.

"A bright spot in your story."

"It was all bright for me. I loved your voice. I thought you were Chekhov, but handsome."

Gallin was easily flattered, and comparisons to that sagacious fellow physician, must flatter even the immune. That Ana revived this moment in their surprisingly mutual past—he was knocked out by it, thrilled. The story made it seem that they had had a relationship all along.

They stood at the window a long time, talking and looking out, the final streaks of daylight bending in the sky. They talked more about the masks. Tell me what drew you to that one, she demanded, pointing to the table. What did you love about this face first, she asked, pointing to one on the floor. She was ardent; she was sharp. Only then did Gallin consider her age, surprising since it was normally the first thing he noted. Before height, race, anything else, he registered a person's age. An occupational hazard, he thought. Considering it now, he saw that her once surely dominating beauty had faded slightly. She possessed a vigor that in others would have signified youth, but that in her had the opposite effect. At its peak hers had surely been a slow, languorous beauty—and the slightly anxious vigor told the tale of its departure.

Gallin thought there was something about her that indicated she had been through something, something big, and now was on the other side of it. Free, as it goes. Suddenly he felt the same.

"I lost my son," he said to her.

"I know," she said. "I'm sorry."

"I don't know why," he said, and shook his head absently. "Why I lost him."

They were both still facing the window.

"I lost my husband," she said.

"I'm sorry," Gallin replied. "The one from whom you got the name Garibaldi?" he asked. "It doesn't seem like a name you'd have started out with. I'm sorry—I'm just curious."

"No, it's all right, it's fine." She didn't move, but somehow she seemed to look further out into the darkness coming on. "My family was from Syria. I was married to Antonio Garibaldi, the painter. You could know his name."

Gallin didn't. He wished he did. But he sensed keenly that it didn't matter. He felt a warmth between them as they stood there. In the warmth was forgiveness for what they did not know.

"He killed himself."

"Oh, I'm sorry."

"It's okay. I think now that it's okay." She looked at him. "He had to. He was in too much pain. He had no reality. He was in an asylum in London—a five-alarm manic depressive."

It was a strange gesture for him, to move his hand without looking, in search of hers. But it felt natural, automatic, innocent. Their fingers clasped, softly. Then she squeezed his hand.

"I have a son," she said quietly, aware that this was something he could no longer say. "He's an art student at UCLA. Paints like his father. You should see the work. You would like it."

"I'm sure I would."

"He's got great command of these colors," she said, lifting their clasped hands together to indicate the exhausted orange, the dappled silver, the dark maroon of dusk. "These last light shades."

An hour later they had sex in the darkness of the bedroom, as the evening became night. Both of them were hungry for it. Gallin thought it was like the sex of teenagers, an act so consuming it eclipsed the world beyond it totally. He was desperate to touch her everywhere, and she was luxuriant to the touch—feline, melting, ageless, happy.

The sound that woke them was definitive: there was someone in the house. The intruder had knocked over something in the living room out by where the masks lay on the table. It's Adams, Gallin thought. He's out of his mind. Gallin put his hand over Ana's mouth, then pulled it away slowly, to show her rather cinematically that it would be a bad idea to scream. He slipped on his trousers and slid a small pine box out from under the bed. He took a loaded .38 caliber pistol from it.

Gallin drew a quick sketch in his mind of the redhead, looking for a clue that might have forewarned him of this. But even redrawn, Adams didn't seem capable of a break-in; he seemed like nothing more than a gay thug, looking for some nickels.

Screwy fucking nutcase—now he's gone over the edge. I should have thrown him out with a baseball bat the first time. What was I doing listening to him on the phone? I encouraged him. Gallin prepared himself mentally to shoot, though he still believed in his gut that Adams—even an Adams in his living room—was not a real threat. Maybe it was because Adams's anger was justifiable. Gallin would be angry about Peter too, if he were Adams. Justifiable anger, being born of reason, scared him less.

Gallin moved into the hallway, stepping toward the living room in the dark, hugging the walls. "Who's there?" he asked gruffly, not quite shouting. "Who's there?" he demanded.

He took another couple of steps, almost to the edge of the hallway.

"Adams?" he called out. "Adams, don't do anything stupid. Or whoever you are. Whoever you are I'm telling you—you really shouldn't be here. I've got a gun."

The light flashed on in the living room, blinding Gallin momentarily. He raised the pistol. Blinking he saw a tall bearded man in a baseball hat standing against the far wall holding one of the masks. It was broken in half. Flustered—flushed with adrenaline, with fear and anger, high from having just made love—Gallin didn't quite understand what he saw. He thought he might vomit. The man in front of him was familiar, but the moment seemed to be happening in a dream.

"Don't shoot," the man said, in a voice that drove through Gallin's heart. The man dropped both halves of the mask to the floor. "Don't shoot Dad, it's me."

It was Bernardo. Good god. He was alive.

SEVEN

One can never grip the clouds, and even the touched-down rainbows resist us. The sun, nearest star to wish on, grants life but would as soon flay it. And that star's outré cousins make a mockery of time: gone before we see them, their twinkling just a legacy of exhaustion. Such is the gorgeous, upending illogic of the sky, hope's last redoubt, where time ticks in helices. Where invented gods swagger and preen. Where our dead—the deserving, at least—defy mortality: flying up among the glittery gases even as we bury them in the earth. So heaven, then: forty black-eyed virgins, St. Peter's pat on the back, or some ripe steamy isle like Eden. Of paradise, versions vary, but never location. It's up, always, where time peels back.

So when Bernardo dropped in from the sky, from beyond, Gallin embraced him as though he had clutch of time itself. He pressed against his son's immortal cheek; his gun fell to the floor. He kissed his scruffy resurrected neck, breathed in his sour smell, and held on tight. And what he thought was this: maybe I, too, will never die.

Visions of a young Bernardo blew across his mind like a slide show: the boy at two gaining intimate knowledge of a spoon; at three turning over a cup of water again and again in the bath, learning gravity; at age five in the Cathedral of St. John the Divine in Morningside Heights one weekday afternoon, sweetly asking his father to marry him, *the same way you married pretty Mommy,* said the boy—and the two of them walking the long aisle in a mock processional, solemn and nervous, holding hands beneath the voluptuous organ music being practiced a bit too fiercely above, and pledging to each other: *till death do us part*—the motherless child already knowing too much about death and parting. Then there was the sun-browned Bernardo swimming in the lake at Woodbrook, sixteen perhaps, and this a shimmering split-memory of himself too at the same age, his own body lithe and wet and reaching still with that deep-coded force for its eventual height: that golden season of life when it—the body, the sun, the water, the world—was all beautiful.

He tightened his embrace. The visions came in bunches, in schools—fish stories of a life. Gallin tried to catch them, but they tumbled over the falls. What river ran below the plummet of memory? Where did it flow? Bernardo's quiet breath, labored as it was squeezed out of him by his father, exploded in Gallin's lupine ear like thunder.

"Dad, I need you to do something for me," he said. "I need two things, actually. I need your help."

A<small>T EIGHT</small> in the morning on September 11, 2001, Bernardo Gallin had stood smoking a cigarette near the edge of the vast World Trade Center plaza, a few hundred yards from the Towers. He wore a dark suit, a crisp white shirt, and an expensive silver tie. If he was examining his life, it was none too strenuously. Rather, he was enjoying the moment. The sky was marvelously blue, the morning placid and cool, and the air felt particularly fresh as it swallowed up his exhalations.

In fact, Bernardo had worked hard to kick the habit of self-examination, having determined that it caused nothing but turmoil. Even though the smoking put him in a contemplative mood—especially that first sensual smoke of the day, which seemed to shake the mind's other poisons into action—he was careful to look outward and not in, thereby avoiding much potential conflict.

Had any of his colleagues seen him smoking, it's safe to say they would have been shocked. For Bernardo had cultivated a reputation of masterly efficiency and order, out from which a louche smoking habit would have stuck like a tail from a bird.

That very morning when he lit his smoke he had already put in three hours at his desk. Indeed, for seven-and-a-half straight years—since his graduation with an MBA from the University of Florida—Bernardo had arrived at the offices of Bentley & Partners at five-thirty AM, Monday through Friday, snow, pregnancy, hangovers, houseguests, and self-doubt notwithstanding. It was an audacious display of personal industry, even by the rigorous standards of the money industry—and he had got his reward.

He had made almost a half million dollars in each of the two previous years while doing little more than going along, as one can do in a good position, like a rider drafting in the Tour de France. But six months before, he'd made a springtime score with a prescient suggestion about Euro futures that netted the firm fifty-one million dollars in fees, and thrust him personally into the serious eight-figure strata—even as hyper-extended highfliers in other firms were getting peppered by the bursting NASDAQ bubble. He used the money for the down payment on a four-bedroom penthouse on Park Avenue at 92nd Street with a view of Central Park. He was looking forward to watching the leaves change color in the fall.

He lived in this apartment with his wife, Kiran, an artist pretty much uninjured by the mean demands of commercial success, and his infant son, Tyler. Or rather those two lived in the apartment and Bernardo visited briefly in the evenings. At least that was how it felt. He was no longer in love with his wife, and felt strangely ambivalent about the boy.

These facts he understood as he smoked that morning but he tried, as always, not to think of them. Part of the deal he had made with himself precluded his delving too deeply into the muck of emotion, where he had seen so many people, most especially his father, founder and suffer. The tragic held no romance for him.

Bernardo had gotten into some trouble as a young man. There was a lot of cocaine around, which had chiefly the effect of obscuring how much pot he was smoking and how much liquor he consumed. Anyway that—and a charmer's belief that society's emphasis on discipline was surely mislaid—was how he'd ended up down in Florida for school, when his father's connections and his own cleverness should have easily paved his way through one of those storied Ivy League institutions whose star football players would get their asses kicked by the Gators' water boy. And while he didn't regret his choices—not entirely anyway—if he allowed himself he felt an opportunity had been lost. Had he gone to Yale or Princeton he might have been a playwright or something like that—something individual. Even a failed playwright who was out of Yale could claim some incontrovertible dignity.

But because he did not follow that path, he'd put himself in the rotten position of having his proving ground constantly beneath his feet. Or so he believed. Fresh out of bed each morning he'd step on that proving ground again, never having bothered to secure it, as many did, by the time he was seventeen. For an Upper East Side rich kid to end up kicking the undergrad books down at Gainesville said certain things about him—none of which was positive when it came to pursuing a career earning money in black socks.

It was in his junior year—after two-plus years of continued juvenile debauchery in the Florida sunshine—when he finally sensed the potential peril of having forsaken his advantages, and what this meant for his future. Of course, a Yale degree had less to do with education than with position and perception—of that he was convinced. Nevertheless, he realized he would have to make up for having missed getting one and he needed to create a plan to compensate. It was a late wake-up call but a loud one.

The very afternoon this need occurred to him he sat down in the coffee shop on campus and made a list of adults he knew, mostly his father's friends. He divided them into two groups. At the top of the first column he wrote NEAT and at the top of the second, after struggling to come up with the term, he wrote untidy. He wrote the latter sloppily for effect. Between the two, in parenthesis, he wrote (LIFE).

Thirty-one names filled the lists, about evenly divided. The first name he filled in on the untidy side was *Richard Gallin, M.D.* His father's life was a study in untidy. A charming man, he relied on charm. Indeed, as Bernardo built his columns, the untidy section grew fat with charming men—and women too, occasionally, just as those who filled the NEAT column were mostly devoid of charm. They were fine people, those listed under NEAT: they were upstanding, honest, dignified, reliable, successful, and generous. But they lacked the looseness and fluidity, the naturally commiserative compassion that was charm's essence. In other words, they were straight. When a name belonging in the NEAT column popped up it tended to place itself there immediately. If a name required any real deliberation, untidy it was. The NEAT, upon appearing in mind, got directly in line. Untidy equivocated.

It was a surprise to discover that charm was the linking characteristic of all those untidy lives—shared by a singer, a glass artist, entrepreneurs, a judge, investment bankers, a music agent, a publisher, a producer, and a couple of restaurateurs. The sculptor Sudol, who made the perfectly balanced glass shapes and was on his fifth marriage, was put down second on the list, just below his father. Bernardo thought of five charming untidys before the first NEAT occurred to him. Charm, he saw, was a boomerang: those who practiced it were also susceptible. Sipping his coffee he vowed never to be a victim of it. So it followed that neither must he continue to rely on it. He checked his list and saw how reliance on charm would be easy to fall into—almost everyone in the untidy column had made a life of it. These were colorful and in some ways enviable lives. But they were filled with divorces and reversals, heartache and hatred, betrayals and disintegration—too much to pay for the occasionally great, but too often debilitating thing called passion.

A larger problem still was that charm was not real; it could not be quantified. Charm was merely the adroit reading of and reacting to situations. It was always ephemeral, never tangible. It depended for existence on the moment it was in—a performer's art, constructed from insecurity. And because Bernardo was an adept he needed to be especially careful. If one spent it as currency, one must also accept it. Bernardo decided it would be easier not to.

He decided that he would place his life firmly into the NEAT column, even if he had to subjugate all his natural urges, to sublimate his intrinsic self. He knew it could be done because in most great stories that was the hero's journey—the hero transcends his circumstances to become another, better man. Bernardo decided that afternoon to be, above all, respectable, a man of dignity—unshakably in the NEAT. Neat, neat, neat.

He set his course. And outwardly, his metamorphosis was a success.

So it was one of his secrets that the early bird approach to work was a ruse, one component in the elaborate artifice he'd built to disguise the fact that he was not, by nature, of Type-A temperament, like his Bentley colleagues. They fell naturally into the NEAT. In truth, Bernardo was conspicuous among Bentley bigwigs in *not* thinking that the world was his oyster, that the sun rose and set with him, and that his success and achievement were inevitable. Instead, naturally he fretted, he worried. He considered ambiguity. But he put this aside.

Still at times he felt like a robin, flitting between unwavering oaks. The NEATs were so assured, so unbending. In secrecy he longed to be like them, to make his performance permanent. But the very act of longing precluded his ultimate transformation. The NEATs did not long. Still, the more he went through the motions of certitude—the more he mimicked their insouciance, their entitlement—the more powerful grew his urge to join their kind. Yet to his sinking disappointment, he was not converted. He wondered if others had truly managed it—conversion? People were always trying. He knew his own was incomplete because he sometimes felt sad, which was something it seemed they did not. He saw them become angry or appalled, but never sad.

"Pretend to be a thing all your life," his father had told him once, talking about courage, "and at the end of your life that's what you'll have been—the thing you pretend to be."

"But then who are you?"

"Act as if you're brave and you'll be brave."

Bernardo straddled the columns, and felt satisfied, if not happy.

Gifted in subterfuge though he was, Bernardo was nevertheless surprised to discover how little it took to be mistaken for one of the NEAT. Dark shoe polish, an excellent tie, punctuality—that was near holiness—and a sharp ear for the direction others thought things were headed—the recipe for deception was not longer than this. Oh, and he was heedful to stay on the heavy side physically, especially in the face, in order to project a stolid personal architecture. Lean and hungry, like Cassius, would not serve. (There were some in the NEAT who included a fastidious physical fitness in their armature, but this vanity was secretly suspect to the others, who saw in the fascination with self-improvement an inherent disrespect for the status quo.)

At any rate, as for where things were headed, at least in business, people always gave themselves away. Indeed, the higher one climbed the more information one was given, as the desire of people to be thought brightest of the bright consistently trumped discretion. A secret-keeper was a rare, rare thing.

While there were a few uncommonly smart operatives in the fold, most of the strivers at Bentley & Partners simply squeezed on formal systems until they found an exploitable imbalance—a loophole, a fissure, a flaw. One was always there. The miniscule variance in skill between the equally educated Bentley flaw-finders led to the information giveaway, because the only way to distinguish one's self was by publicizing one's views. Add to this a disinclination to be alone out on the limb and there it was. Risk, as much as misery, loved company. So Bernardo learned that if you hung around enough someone would usually point you to what they'd found—just to prove to you that they saw it. That's why he got there early.

Bentley operated, as did most American finance, on the supposition that the world of commerce law was the beat-up, labyrinthine, and totally temporary result of good intentions, shortsightedness, and other unbreakable habits of a distracted bureaucracy. Charting a course through the logistical aberrations in the system was, in a nutshell, the service the firm provided its clients. Herculean companies ranging from the Bank of America to the now bottomed-out Enron bought this service at incredible prices, essentially financing the research and then on average splitting the take with Bentley, the navigator. Finance, always a predatory game, had been fed virtual amphetamines by the information age. Companies had to be in constant motion. Bentley's great skill was to convey funds—which companies, to Bernardo's surprise, often handled clumsily—so that they were exposed to the least regulatory and competitive friction. In a single day last summer they'd bilked the Canadian government out of $160 million in tax revenues by moving two billion dollars through seven entities in an hour. It was all legal. And as far as Bernardo was concerned it was ethical. Everybody at Bentley got a new Swiss watch.

The cigarette tasted especially fine. Smoking was one of his few remaining refuges in the world of untidy. He loved to watch the masses of people streaming up from underground, coming from every kind of home imaginable—the rat race. He loved to witness their collective glory—being both one of them and, for a moment, out on this edge of it, apart. The glamour of Wall Street was really these hordes, their dreams and their battles against obscurity.

The percolating morning rush—he loved especially to watch those women who still sported with trudging dignity the now venerable uniform of sneakers, skirts, and high-hair from the '80s—when Wall Street was Michael Milken and Drexel and Michael Douglas and greed is good and the movie *Working Girl* with Melanie Griffith in her garter belt and high-teased coif. Change was in some ways an illusion. They kept coming and coming, the ambitious. What machines you could power with only the static electricity in their clothes! Bernardo was mesmerized by the compoundedness of it all. The *productivity*. The worker productivity number was due out on Thursday and it was a figure investors like him watched carefully. But there was something about the number that felt very last-century, that needed some real reworking before it could reveal any truth. Unlike the interest rate and housing starts, the productivity number was something investors didn't quite know how to react to anymore. Productivity, long a benchmark of progress, had a certain gloom to it these days: it reeked of robots and third-world labor, of an efficiency that dehumanized. It was getting harder to say unequivocally that more productivity was good. It might mean fewer workers, for one.

No doubt though, we were productive. All one had to do was stand where Bernardo stood to see it: this fantastic amusical march of the bedraggled militia of capitalism, with its astoundingly complex assembly line of phone-callers, meeting-takers, keyboardists, plant-waterers, vacuumers, electricians, shopkeepers, waitresses, bartenders, burger flippers, security guards and thieves that was Wall Street, a city inside a city, the real capital of the world. What did Deep Throat say? *Follow the money.*

Bernardo took a deep drag. He arched his back and craned his neck—the blue sky filled his eyes. What a glorious blue, he thought again. What a marvelous sky. It was strange to consider that his office was up in it—up in the sky. They had really outdone themselves with ambition, building these towers. Then that Frenchman, the daredevil, had outdone even the builders and gone and walked between them on a wire. That was amazing. Bernardo wished he had seen that. It was really unimaginable. We were always outdoing one another. What would be next? He painted a weak little cloud on the blue with his smoke; it wafted up and disappeared. Then he heard the roaring. It tore at his ears. And he was staring at the underbelly of the jet when its nose ripped through his office window.

At first, he ran toward the building. But then it occurred to him that everyone in his office was definitely dead.

AT THE top of Gallin's townhouse, the wind strengthened. It wailed against the brick, and slapped rhythmically against the windows like a ship's wake against a moored dinghy. The townhouse creaked, its century-old joints contracting, moaning at winter.

Gallin let go and stepped back to regard his son. From the high crest of shock his emotions surfed raggedly down. He was lightheaded with glee. An almost religious gratitude welled up in him—he curved toward the earth with it: then the wave crashed in a foam of anger. There was salt in his mouth. But the brackish anger slid away too, leaving him feeling naked, in dumb awe. His skin sagged. He counted his years.

Released, Bernardo walked matter-of-factly toward the cabinets above the countertop, on which the afternoon's teacups still sat faintly redolent and forlorn. He opened a cabinet—just as if he hadn't risen from the dead—and pulled down a box of wheat crackers. He dug deep for a fistful, shoving about half the load in his mouth at once. He took off his jacket—a heavy black leather thing—and threw it onto the back of the sofa. Gallin thought he remembered the move, full of adolescent nonchalance. Might Bernardo have performed it regularly as a boy—a tiny after-school revolt, the refusal to hang up his jacket? It seemed like a trustworthy memory, but he wasn't sure. In fact, he began to doubt all the visions—the whole show—that he'd just entertained in his mind. Were those Bernardo or some figment? What is real, he asked himself. Silently he begged the universe to tell him. Gallin could see the boy's shape was changed: his middle was thin. He couldn't think of what to say, and the boy seemed in no hurry to speak.

He must stop, he knew, thinking of Bernardo as a boy. That had been one of the hard things in mourning him—mourning the loss of a child. A man, a man can die. That's what a man does. But considering one's children as adults, even after they have children of their own, was hard to accomplish. Gallin never even had the will to try.

He looked again at his son; suddenly he experienced an eruption of shame. He may vomit yet. He bit hard on his teeth to hold it back.

Bernardo sat down with the box of crackers in his lap. Then he stood up again, as if the sofa had been red hot, and put the box down on the countertop. He took a half-minute to finish chewing. He swallowed hard and Gallin saw again how truly thin he was, the ravenous chewing making a point of it, the Adam's

80

apple bulging in his throat. Gallin remembered the useless fact that it takes twenty-five muscles to swallow. Had Bernardo been taken prisoner? But he realized almost before the question was formed that there had been no prisoners. Not even the bombers, of course, lived.

Bernardo wore blue jeans, which hung on him only by being belted snugly around the hips. He wore a white t-shirt, nothing more, under the big leather jacket, the black bulk of which lay thuggish against the soft caramel-colored sofa. Something in the way the two leathers touched suggested rape. He must have dropped thirty pounds, even forty, Gallin thought. Bernardo was six feet one, but now he could weigh only 160, 165. Tops. Gallin took in the spectre of him. His cheekbones protruded handsomely, severely. He was also tanned; he had been in the sun. His green eyes, which he lifted from his mother, looked back with a prepossessing clarity. They had a savage glint. Bernardo's face looked more or less like his own: a long straight nose that would have been at home in the Roman Senate, the thoughtful half-moon of forehead, the plump bottom lip—great indicator of sensuality— that Bernardo had always seemed for some reason to hold in, to purse—these features belonged to both men. But the eyes were alarming. They had changed. Gallin's own were brown and intelligent, a little quick and wary. After all, he had secrets.

Bernardo's eyes, though, were alien. In his wife's pale face they had been a gorgeous, enchanting green. But replanted in Bernardo's darker skin—Gallin's gift—these eyes were slack and unnerving. Gallin had always thought his son's eyes were wrong, wrongly placed—a rare circumstance where nature had made a poor selection. But now as he faced them this no longer seemed true. The formerly contrary green fit better now with his lean face. That was it! These were hungry eyes—just as they had been in Christa—and they had not matched Bernardo before. They had not suited him. Wherever he had been, whatever he had seen since September 11th, Bernardo seemed to have become himself. He fit his own eyes now. He looked like one of those pictures of the saints. Will that happen to me? Gallin wondered. When I die will I look like a saint? He turned from Bernardo for a moment to face himself in the glass. He was struck by the massive size of his loneliness. It seemed to extend beyond his body like a force field. He felt as he did when a doctor took his pulse, the two fingers pressed against his throat, the silent count during that long terrifying minute, when one understands above all that there is a limit on heartbeats.

The wind knocked over an empty wine bottle on the terrace. It sounded a high, tinkling note, then rolled abysmally.

"You've got to explain this, explain yourself," Gallin said. "To say the least. Are you all right?"

"What a question, but yes, I would say I am all right."

"Explain, Bernardo. Wait." Gallin walked over and poured himself a cognac. "You want one of these?"

"No. No thank you."

Gallin poured himself a good size drink.

"This is quite a trick, son, coming back from the dead. A bad prank? Very bad."

He walked over and sat down on the chair beside the sofa. He wanted to say, "hang up your jacket" and treat the night as some other, normal night. He took a deep breath.

"Have you been to see your wife and child?" he asked. There was a long pause. "You should start talking now."

Bernardo stood for a moment by the windows, looking out. He bent down and picked up the gun from the floor, regarding it with no more gravity than he would a dog toy. He put it in the cabinet where he had got the wheat crackers.

"I can't explain," he said. "And I don't need to. I came here because I need your help and that's that. I'm not coming back to my life here. I've been released from it."

He took some newspaper from his back pocket and unfolded it. It was a full page from the *New York Times*.

"By the way," he said, "You living should be ashamed of this." He held the paper out in front of him. "This was disgusting."

You living, Gallin repeated to himself. By that had Bernardo meant to implicate everyone? *You living*. What an oddity. Gallin, however intrinsically pleased to be part of the group, was confused. Bernardo was alive, too, right in front of him, though by his phrase he seemed to exclude himself. But no matter what side of the divide Bernardo stood on, still, god, what a category! The living! Who had named such a group before? And of course the living should be ashamed. Weren't they? And who was Bernardo—who was anybody—to indict us all? What did they have in common, after all, these living? The whole burning, bleeding, stinking, stealing, lying, loving lot of them—what could they share? That's a crock of shit, Gallin thought. I'm not going to stand for being put in that group . . .

"I've been released and I can start over and I'm going to. And that's what I need you for, Dad. Here's my release, officially." He looked at the newspaper. "This is from the Portraits in Grief section. Thank god there aren't any other dead besides me to read these little remembrances and see how puny our lives were. The living are so arrogant."

"Bernardo, we're—I—I'm going to get you some help. You are in some kind of shock."

"Listen to this," Bernardo continued. " 'Lucy Rocuski loved cats. "Everyone knew she loved cats and so when Lucy's birthday came around it was like a feline festival—so many kitten cards and stuff," said Tina, her best friend. Ms. Rocuski had a bright smile. "Every day when you saw Lucy, you knew there was someone in the world who cared. You knew there were more important things in life" said a former coworker.'

"More important things than what?" Bernardo asked aloud. "They're all like this. Loved cats, loved dogs, loved to party, loved to golf, had a bright smile, offered a kind word for everyone, loved family, loved hamburgers—that's all they say. A real life in fifty words or less, maybe a hundred. It's criminal. Better they stay silent. The editors of this paper should be murdered, and then get a paragraph each about how they loved their BMWs."

"Where have you been?"

"Do you want to hear mine?"

"I want to know where you've been. I want to help you."

"You know what it says about me?"

"Yes, I do. I know what it said."

"It says that I was early. That it was the secret to my success—you know Ben Franklin crap. Early to bed, early to rise. That's it. Thirty-one years. That's it."

"Bernardo, I didn't talk to anyone at the paper."

"Thank you."

"I'll ask you again: have you been home?"

"You know what, though? It's true. They're right. I was early. That's what I *was*."

Impatient, but determined to remain calm, Gallin asked again. "Bernardo, have you been home?"

"No. I went down to Florida after the attacks and I've been here just a couple of days. I've got to get out of here fast though. I've been laying low but someone will see me. I saw Dr. Rhodes over by the museum just after I got to the city. That made it clear I don't have much space here. I had on a hat and sunglasses, but he looked like he recognized me. He sort of waved. Listen, Dad, I need you to do surgery on me. I can't be recognized by anybody. I need you to."

"Bernardo, you're in some kind of shock. You need—"

"Look at me," Bernardo replied, his voice challenging. "I *survived* it. I'm a *miracle*. Don't tell me what I need, Dad. I was killed. I was *dead*. So now I'm free."

Gallin stared down into the snifter on his knee; he swished the brandy around.

"But your wife and son—your responsibilities," he said softly, still looking down, as if a list of a man's responsibilities could be conjured from the swishing.

"I didn't quit them. I didn't quit or just leave. I was released. What are my responsibilities, really? I've fulfilled them. Kiran and Tyler are set for life financially. The firm paid out, plus the insurance, plus the government giving out the "we-fucked-up-sorry" money. They're set. Set for life. I've covered my responsibilities."

"What about different kinds of responsibilities? What about your life—what you built—don't you want it?"

"It wasn't me. It wasn't mine. It was manufactured."

"Son, everybody feels that way a little bit. It doesn't mean it's not genuine—it's just—what about your wife?"

"That was over. She's better off, too."

"And your son. Tyler will need you. You're a father."

"It's not a disaster to have only one parent, Dad," Bernardo replied.

Despite himself Gallin was lifted by this answer, assuaged.

"Dad, it's simple. I need two things. You're the only one who can help me. I need the surgery so I can truly start again. And you're right about one thing—I need you to help me see Tyler. Just one more time. Just for a minute. I want to see how it feels to see him."

Gallin looked up at the man in front of him. "I don't know what to say."

"You don't have to know the answers. You don't have to know my reasons at all—only that they're mine. I have them. I'm your son. Help me. I need it done this week. I can't stay."

Neither spoke for minutes, until Bernardo moved over and sat down on the sofa's edge, near his father's chair. He put his hand on Gallin's knee. "Dad," he said, "this is real."

Gallin's ear fumbled the word. Wasn't that what he had begged the universe to tell him? Just moments ago? What was real? And back from the dead comes his only son to say this, this is it? This is what's real? Mercy, Gallin beggared. This was how religion happened. These forces, these questions, these choices—too large for a man.

"Where will you go?" he asked.

"I'm not sure. West, I think. Oregon, maybe."

"How will you live? What will you do?"

"I don't know. I hope the right thing."

More silence, more wind.

"Wouldn't you do it, Dad? I mean if you could, wouldn't you start over again?"

Gallin closed his eyes.

"I can't change the way you look very much," he said. "Superficial changes really. You'll still look like you."

"You can do a lot. I've seen it. You did that thing for the CIA for a while."

"FBI. Only so much can be changed. Honestly."

"You know what to do, Dad. No one's better."

"I have to think, Bernardo." He reached out and cupped Bernardo's cheek in his palm. They looked eye to eye. Gallin was comfortable with the eyes now, with the man whose face he held. "Don't do it, I want to say."

"I'm already gone, Dad. It's just a question of whether you'll help me. If it's you or someone else."

Gallin looked down at his chest; he thought his heart might fly out of it. "Okay," he said. Then he said it again but there was no sound, just a pocket of air.

"Thank you, Dad," Bernardo said and gripped his father's face too, pulled his cheek against his cheek. His wet eye touched against his father's ear, which was heavy. "Thank you," he repeated.

BEHIND GALLIN'S bedroom door, Ana Garibaldi sat on the floor listening. She was in tears herself and, for the moment, forgotten.

EIGHT

Monday morning Nick Adams stood on the corner of 73rd & Lexington, bouncing on the balls of his feet. His sinewy frame shook with malevolent energy. The morning air was mild and moist—the wind having exhausted itself during the night— yet despite this clemency Adams gave the appearance of a man trying to keep warm. He blew in his hands and rubbed them together. Again he went up on his toes. Adrenaline pushed him around; it jolted his muscles: it surged through his body like love.

Only Friday his efforts to avenge his lover—to exact retribution from the rich doctor who had callously cast dear Peter aside— hinged weakly on the thinnest premise. The "you could have AIDS" gambit was, he knew, exactly as Gallin assessed it: preposterous. Even had it been true—and Gallin was an HIV carrier—still there was no protocol requiring him to be tested. At any rate, it was clear that the accusation did not constitute a good enough story to publish. Not in *New York* magazine, not anywhere. Even before September 11th such a gossamer indictment would have keeled over after its first weak whimper; after the 11th it would arrive stillborn on the editor's desk, with no hope of ink amidst the tragedy/terrorism din. And without a looming publication date, what kind of threat was an exposé? Adams should have aborted it early, but he kept hoping the doctor would blink and allow even such a toothless accusation to have its effect, to bend him back. After all, Adams knew a good deal about Gallin by this time, and he surmised from his research that his target must be low. Reports were of sullenness and lost bearings. Of erratic behavior. Even Adams had been able to keep him unaccountably on the phone during those prolonged instances of silent faceless dialogue that had frankly spooked them both. So the hunter continued to hope that his folly would work—right up until the moment on Friday when he confronted Gallin. The doctor did not seem sufficiently shaken or alarmed.

It was frustrating because for months Adams had thrown all his reportorial acumen toward the goal of leveling his adversary. Adams's love for his waylaid lover Peter—the first pure, uncomplicated love he had ever experienced—was only a part of his animus, for Adams had an aggrieved sense of justice to begin with. His biography was a mountain of hellish circumstance. Gallin's aloofness was just a match to a fuse.

Born in South Boston twenty-seven years before, Adams was the child of a rape. The mother was fourteen. She wanted desperately to abort, but caught in the holy safety net of the local Jesuits she became reluctant to choose eternal damnation. Since all acts, including rape, must be the will of God, giving birth was the proper thing to do. It would protect her from His wrath.

The wrath of God, she was told by her comforters, was something—just like his goodness, my dear—that is so powerful we can never understand it. It was obviously something to be avoided. We must simply trust in God's plan, dear girl, she was told, and the Way shall become clear to us. The young girl prayed for forgiveness. She had known her attacker, albeit slightly, and this fact softened, in the Jesuit minds, the barbarism of the rape. What was never explicitly said was that in the eyes of the church her having known her rapist made her vaguely complicit. She was a victim therefore not entirely without blame. We were all sinners, of course. If it had been a big black man—someone foreign—instead of a young drunken Irish from the neighborhood, then she could have laid indisputable claim to blamelessness. But as it stood there was always the infuriating question of whether she mightn't have acted with a little more propriety. Not been so provocative, girl?

The rape had been a brutal one, and the child made her sick when she held it. She gave it up. Later she was a suicide.

The infant Adams disappeared into the maze of care and corruption, prayer and profit, provided by the diocese in cooperation with the city. It was hard-knock, Oliver Twist stuff, and his homes were temporary and many. Even so, it had its lowlights. When he was twelve, a priest named Flaherty took him from the orphanage and drove him to see his father, who had gone after prison to live in New Hampshire. They arrived at a shack to find his rapist father dead on the floor, poisoned by alcohol. Dead about six hours by four in the afternoon, the coroner later informed them. The young Adams was not as disturbed by the strange man's being dead, though, as by his being fat. Earlier, in reaction to a violent Creationist nun who had beat him, Adams had developed a powerful devotion to Darwinism. He was determined to be among the fittest. So the corpulent genealogy he saw prone and flabby on the floor in the form of his father aggrieved him. From then on, the potential lurking in him for a loose physiognomy worried his mind.

He was touched sexually beginning at age fourteen by Flaherty, who was gentle, loving and lonely, and who taught him to be the same, and also later by a big burly priest named Schladabach, who smelled like pipe tobacco and boiled carrots.

The priest who saved his soul was Burns, who took him boxing. In the gym he learned hard justice and how to turn out his rage. He was good, too—tough, skinny but dynamic. He won his weight class at the Golden Gloves at sixteen—a national champ. Burns gave him Hurricane Carter's book, about the wrongly accused boxer and his ferocious fight for freedom. Presto: Adams had a hero. Then Burns gave him Hemingway stories to read. It was from these he chose his name, liking the stoic Nick Adams of "Big Two-Hearted River" and "The Killers." After that he read a lot, from Toni Morrison to Joyce Carol Oates, Maugham to Mailer. He was himself, he felt, a prisoner of sex. For a long time he associated sex only with violation. It was hard to escape it: he was born of a massive violation. He was the result of an act that killed the woman and imprisoned the man. Indeed, the idea of a man and a woman having sex disgusted him. Only pain could come of it.

Adams fell in love with Father Burns. In fact, he tried to seduce him, but Burns was not for it. It was Burns who knew a couple of people in New York in the magazine business and got Adams out of town. He left Boston with hot coals burning in his head and his heart, filled with blind want and hunger. It was a hunger for success, for God, for justice, for a world that fit better with what he'd been told.

Gallin's heartless, perfunctory dismissal of Peter—even all these years later only stoked those coals, which had never cooled. Adams had been impressively stolid in his acceptance of Peter's diagnosis. And he had proudly mustered the most serious if deluded kind of courage as well, the one-eyed half-courage it took to remain unquestioning about how the supposedly loyal and clean-when-they-met Peter had contracted the virus. He shooed away that toxic question like a fruit fly, preferring not to know about the transgression that infected him. But in Gallin, who had gone and topped the ignominy of AIDS with the ostracizing dart of unemployment, he found a redressible point of focus for his rage.

Yet the months of research on Gallin had turned up little he could use. He interviewed friends and acquaintances of the doctor, saying by way of introduction that he had been hired by his son, Bernardo, to produce a celebratory biography of the man for his sixtieth birthday. This tugged on heart strings and inspired candid remembrances, especially after Bernardo was killed—with Adams proclaiming gallantly that he was "determined to see the project through." Indeed after the 11th, Adams was able to mine a more general vulnerability in people. Everyone seemed to be writing their own memoirs in mind, and Adams's fake project was a great receptacle for their emotional spillage. Indeed, after so many interviews Adams felt that the dead Bernardo was something like a brother to him, so movingly did people speak when struck loquacious by sympathy. Bernardo seemed like someone who, if you read between the lines, might have hated the doctor too.

Those interviewed were cautioned, of course, not to tell Gallin of their participation: the book was meant to be a surprise. It was a perfect scheme.

90

Two problems, however, emerged with Adams's plan of attack. First, there was not much more to expose in Gallin than the normal failures of a man of his time. And second, the "risky" behavior Adams ultimately decided to try to use as a weapon was hardly a secret. Rather than embarrassment, Gallin seemed to feel pride and something like nostalgia for the more irresponsible aspects of his life. To Adams's chagrin, it was near impossible to shame a man who felt no shame, who had nothing to hide. So Adams attempted to translate Gallin's personal foibles into a charge of professional misconduct. It was tough going. The logic was that his occupation—his proximity to the blood of thousands over the years—increased by a huge order of magnitude the danger to others represented by his personal choices.

But ultimately this strategy held no water. He had tried to seem menacing and present it like a blistering pox, but five minutes after the confrontation he knew he'd blown it. There was nothing there. Afterward, he'd run down the street furious, jabbing his failure in the eye.

It had made him sick to his stomach. Failing at vengeance was the worst of all humiliations.

So the weekend had been a stewing misery, minute by stinging minute. Adams felt powerless. With each pill he watched Peter down from his HIV cocktail, Adams grew more morose, and angrier.

Then at half past six on Monday morning he slipped quietly out of the Murphy bed they shared. He gelled down his red hair, darkening it. He put on a black, well-made suit, a striped shirt, and a bright tie decorated with holographic moons. His good suits were a substitute for a car and a house; they were what he arrived in and lived in. Beyond his clothes, for possessions he counted some books (he had few, having learned the library's graces from the Jesuits), a laptop computer, and a set of sheets with a very high thread count. He'd learned to travel light. Before he'd moved in with Peter, he knocked around from place to place in the Village, trying for the writer's life. He brought these sheets with him like a dowry.

Silently, he blotted on his throat the tiniest touch of Chanel No. 5 and headed to the N train at Union Square. He was up on the East Side before seven. He had a vague plan to confront Gallin. But how? He could just beat the old man, smash him in the head with a Golden Gloves hook. Let that be the end of it. But he had wanted to fight this on higher ground. A fisticuffs win would be a loss, really.

Everything changed when he saw the baseball-hatted, sun-glassed, scruff-bearded figure emerge from Gallin's townhouse just before eight. Or rather everything changed moments later when the connectors in his brain circumvented what he knew, and allowed him to recognize that the emergent figure was Bernardo. Wait, he thought, it couldn't be. Bernardo was dead, long dead. But he reminded himself: we all know things that can't be true and yet they are. Adams had always tried to remain open to the possibilities of the world; it helped him now. Then he realized: *he's going somewhere early!*

Adams had made a composite of Bernardo from his reporting, and knew something about his style. This was really him! God, this was better than he could have ever hoped! The HIV accusation, that crappy toothless threat, was over—Gallin really was complicit and villainous. No more need to stretch the facts. If Bernardo was alive—and he was, no doubt—then this was huge! It was fraud on a grand scale. It was even more—so much more that he couldn't immediately account for what it all meant. It was unthinkable, really. He could crush the man with this.

Bouncing on the corner and waiting, Adams tried to maintain some cool. But it was hard. He had never been so excited. He channeled his movie heroes. He began with the peculiar form of meditation that was talking to oneself in Clint Eastwood's voice. This had an immediate, felicitous effect: it made him feel he had great power in his shoulders. In addition, it kept one from saying too much, which was paramount.

He practiced the dialogue. "Oh (he would say it tersely but casually, as though wearing a six-shooter), Dr. Gallin." And then real Clint-like, hard as a diamond: "A lot's changed since Friday." He would let it linger then, the threat. Let it build in Gallin's mind like Poe's buried heartbeat.

ADAMS WAITED in agitated joy for the next forty minutes, unable to decide what to do. He should go to the house. Janine, Gallin's assistant, had just arrived. He could get in. No, he wouldn't go to the house, where he failed so miserably on Friday. This new confrontation should happen on the street, under that unique umbrella of crowded privacy New York afforded. Adams now had a probable cover story for *New York*—millions had been paid to Bernardo's wife on Park Avenue. Money from the city, insurance, his company . . . God, it was a journalist's dream. What would Gallin pay to keep it quiet? There was no telling. Wouldn't the story be worth even more published? More than Gallin could possibly pay? The story was Adams's brass ring. No more of this slopping around with secondhand news and crappy concerts. How to handle this . . .

Adams was in just this fit of titillation and scheming when Gallin alighted onto his stoop in his new white tennis shoes and bent down cautiously to touch his toes. He groaned. It was a long sequential process, Gallin's bending over. It happened in sections. More and more he seemed to be divided in parts. When we are young we are one whole thing. Old, we are a collection—lungs and liver, teeth and gums, even our skin goes on its own, getting further from the bones. Father died at sixty, Gallin considered, which is about eighty in today's years. Smoked right up till the end, too. Going by that, I should make it to ninety. Two-thirds then—two-thirds of the way through. But as he suffered the stretching, his long fingers only grazed the tops of his ankles. The math could always be wrong.

The new shoes were a comfort, an inspiration to move. He spread his legs akimbo and bobbed down, extending to reach one foot, then the other. He had a plan to walk to the top of the park, clear his head.

When he had gone to his room the night before, Ana, waiting, had reached out for him, and he remembered how hours before he felt so alive with her, and she touched his face in a way that told him without words that she could be trusted. So, perhaps he wouldn't need to worry about her. Anyway he couldn't afford to—there was too much else. He simply hoped he was right.

Across the street the townhouse was still being worked on. Big lumbering men effortlessly tossed slabs of sheetrock up against their shoulders and marched into it. They had gutted the place. Nothing but the façade remained, like a piece of a set built for a play. Laws prevented altering the faces of these buildings. Mandates forced them to live in perpetuity with their history.

Gallin turned his back on the street and set his long body at forty-five degrees. He pressed his hands against the iron latticework of his front door. One at a time, he stretched his calves. Thus limbered, he set out for Fifth Avenue. He got a pretty good stride going, hoping to set free enough endorphins to enter that lucid state where he could think most clearly. That mental state he'd been in just before he'd plowed over Lester Rhodes.

This time Gallin was intensely mindful of pedestrians. Casting his eyes alertly forward, he claimed with bold arm-swinging a wide berth. He made a warning of himself.

Adams followed at a distance for a while, before falling back. He was not yet sure how to play his new hand.

NINE

For the kingdom and the power and the glory are yours, whispered Fifth Avenue to Richard Gallin. Now and forever. He bestrode the world with privilege again. If what he knew now was troubling, was awful, at least he knew it. Ignorance was worse. What a marvel this avenue was. Its great museums held in captivity the very catalogue of livid mortal artifact, blood of a billion hearts, heat of minds—migrations, movements, monuments, isms. The long struggle toward civilization. In the Met alone: Mesopotamian tombs, Ellsworth Kelly squares, Socrates' hemlock rage; the jewels of the Orient, blurry crepuscular lilies, manic self-portraits in blue; Whistler, Bernini, Byzantium; the Saint-Paul-de-Mausole asylum, this born-dying regnum, that late blooming phylum. All this. Fifth Avenue was the great secular cathedral of man.

Alighting on its sidewalk this Monday morning, moving rapidly through the vanishing mist, Gallin felt as if he were the thin pale arm of a beautiful woman, slipping into a long silk glove. He had tried all religions in his lifetime, and kept returning to this one, with its man-made and mutable totems and dogma, and its almost livable canon. The High Secularism of Fifth Avenue. What else could there be? Why choose another God, so evidently cruel? The glove he imagined was elegant, painstakingly sewn, silk with pearl buttons—the kind of glove he had just missed by being born too late. So much was missed, so much gone forever. Had he missed all the elegance, just by being of his generation? No, he had seen the hats men wore before JFK ripped them from their sorry heads, before the milliners threw up their crippled hands in disgust, cursing the future. Those had been elegant, the hats. Was

95

there anything from today the future would long for? The way he longed for the sight of pale-armed women in silk gloves, taking tea and talking of small books?

The root-flushed cobblestones on the park-side sidewalk protruded helter-skelter below his feet like English teeth. He chose his steps carefully—an ankle's graveyard. This tumult of stone gave way in turn to large slabs of smooth concrete as he approached the Met, as one generation's labor and style gave way to another's. He looked up again. Across the avenue the ornate mansions of last century's barons, long passed over to charitable foundations and *bureaus de affaires international*, looked at once small and large, squat vessels of pout and power, like oversized children, their sad superannuated gargoyles gawking fiercely at defeated superstitions.

They were going to have to build more museums, bigger ones. Six billion of us now. What were we, doubling ourselves every fifty years? Even with the Chinese trying to cool it with their one kid policy, there was no stopping it. Gallin had been to China. In a village outside Chengdu, they had brought him a Panda cub that sat on his lap for an hour and kissed him on the ears. He was never happier. The bears were endangered but the people were piling on. The Indians and the Pakistanis—they may as well be cloning, so efficiently did they multiply. Gallin didn't know about the Arabs, but there damn sure seemed to be more and more of them. Black-eyed killers for oil and Allah. Bigger and bigger, more and more, faster, faster.

In Africa, they were dying just as soon as they were being born, half the babies just insurance policies for desperate mothers trying to scratch their names in the earth, to make something that lived beyond them. They were fucking each other like crazy, in the steaming jungles, on the streets, on the cool dirt floors of shacks in the afternoon, out of the unrelenting sun. Nothing else to do. The whole sub-Saharan region was rife with illiterate warlords carrying swords and machine guns, and big-eyed starving children with marvelous white teeth carrying AIDS. There seemed to be no stopping this either. He had gone to Africa too, three times, to fix cleft palates in clinics in Kenya and the Sudan—but it was overwhelming. The dusty kids, the dried-out hope, the dying, the desperation. In Somalia, there was a whole generation—10,000 children—born from rape. You could smell the hatred in their sweat, like sulfur. You fixed the lips but for what? Gallin cared. He really did. But it was hard. And others didn't care at all, clearly, whatever they professed. What was the proper amount to care? To care for those who can't help themselves? It was impossible to say. One reasonable answer was not too much.

Once when Bernardo was about eight he and Gallin were playing catch in Woodbrook, father and son, the American dream. Gallin was wearing a basketball jersey some friends had given him—a Wilt Chamberlain replica, number 13, but with the name Gallin on the back instead of the Dipper's. In the middle of playing, Bernardo asked: "Dad when you die, can I have that shirt?"

One learned that question was wrong, of course. Impolite. But really, what was wrong with it?

Gallin almost tripped but righted himself. The world made it impossible to be honest. Yet still everyone clamored for honesty. TV psychiatrists, self-help sadists, alcoholics-overeaters-anorexics-anonymous: look at yourself, they all said, and tell the truth. As if there was just one.

Gallin picked up his pace. He imagined breaking through the tape, chest thrust forward. But who was defeated? He noticed up ahead the silver banner for the Sudol retrospective, blending beautifully with the disconsolate sky. His heart raced from his speed. He felt strong, and rich—symptoms of contemplation.

He crossed the avenue and stopped in front of the Cooper-Hewitt. Monday: closed. In the garden though, behind the tall iron-barred fence, two of Sudol's large glass pieces stood in bold contrast to the grey masonry and flaxen winter grass. One was a large luminous green sphere, about six feet tall and semi-translucent. It was raised up near the garden's center on a cinderblock pedestal painted bright white. The other was a three-dimensional rectangle of colorless glass, an empty box, perhaps

97

eight feet in length. A coffin? Suspended by fishing line, it gave the impression of floating in the air. The simple shapes, executed so grandly, the striking choice of color and its absence, and Gallin's own history with the artist all combined to move him deeply. He yearned for the simplicity represented by this art. The brightness, the transparency, the integrity of shape. Had Sudol achieved it—such simplicity? Such integrity? Gallin wanted to call and ask him. "It's Richard," he would say, "and I've been staring at your pieces in the garden, through the bars. And I'm proud and I'm moved . . ."

But a moment later Gallin's vigor vanished. Suddenly he felt cold, and tired. A wind kicked up that, because it took him by surprise, alarmed him. He felt too close to things, exposed; he felt he was in danger. His spirit, fired to great heights by the simple frenzy of his motion, crashed. Worse, it seemed to break into pieces. He was in pain. It was a distinct emotional pain, manifest by the sensation that his lung had collapsed. His chest constricted, his heart in peril, next to fall. He bent over, hands on his knees, and the sidewalk lunged up at him, sparkling and gritty. What was this, he demanded. I can't keep being thrown around like this. A goddamn leaf in the wind, a spindle. Give me order. Give me distinctions! His legs shook, while the milky leather of his tennis shoes seemed heavy as marble. Gravity sans gravitas, he thought. His bottom lip quivered. If he kept going up and down like this he would die of the ride, he was certain. In the distance, a bell pealed insistently. Nearby students were released, shuffled, saved.

Summoning a reserve of strength from near his groin he moved forward, as if against a hurricane. He looked back half-expecting to see his footprints, as if the concrete on which he'd stood had just been poured. No, it was hard as his heart. He trudged on. Again he picked up speed and with sustained velocity he started to feel better, freer. But if he had to keep moving just to hold himself together—well, he couldn't do it. He had a lot of mileage on him already. Good lord, he exclaimed aloud. Let me rest! Just one moment of nothing and I'll be fine. But the world pushed in—*nothing comes of nothing*—and Gallin had a vivid vision of cutting open Bernardo's face.

By the big pond at the northeast corner of Central Park, at 110th Street, he sat down on a bench facing south. This far uptown the din of the city was muted. The new wind whipped up little wavelets that tumbled against the tiny shore. The huge rugged rocks behind the pond gave him something hard and natural to fixate on. Sixty feet high, they were changeless. Ah, time. To himself he said: I am a rock. And then: I am an island. The old Paul Simon lyrics hummed childishly in his brain—a solipsist's clarion call.

He could have used a brother or sister—to mark his time with. His parents should have thought of that. How he would love a brother to talk to. It occurred to Gallin that he had loved his parents; they were good people who had treated him with kindness and respect. And they had meant it. He hadn't known how rare that was. Those two things—kindness and respect—made a man, gave him dignity. But it was hard, through the haze of years, to remember those generous people. Thirty years gone, his parents were little more than an emotion now, little more than a pulse he assigned them, itself as evocative and distorting as a photo, bending fact as gravity bent light. With a brother he might have discussed these things.

Now it felt like a storm blowing in, a squall churning in the west. He gazed at the Empire State Building, surprised that he could see it from this distance, its silver hypodermic tip rising above the web of grey denuded treetops. Sitting, shivering a little, Gallin looked at the skyscraper's thrusting needle and thought, what a world—with all its creating and destroying. He wrapped his arms around himself. As he looked across the pond again into the rocks, tears welled in his eyes for the second time in so many hours—more tears than had escaped him in years. Was he a failure? As a father? As a man?

Not yet, he determined.

The future was a powerful notion.

In Gallin's empty office, Janine picked up the phone and a few seconds later rolled her eyes at Annie. She sighed and started writing.

In a moment the pad in front of her read:

    To: Dr. Gallin
    From: Nick Adams
    Message: I know about Bernardo.

"Thank you, sir, I'll be sure he gets it," she said with sarcastic courtesy.

She wondered if she should really leave this message. What good could come of it, she asked herself. But he had just said to take all messages, and she felt her obligation keenly. She slipped it into his slot.

"Let's get out of here," she said to Annie. They had spent the last hour cancelling his upcoming appointments.

That morning he'd given them the rest of the week off.

GALLIN FOUND the note at noon when he returned from his episode in the park. He recoiled on seeing it: how could he know? Bernardo hadn't been careful. That changed things, certainly.

Passed through the brass mail slot in the door was another message also, wrapped in a small cream-colored linen envelope, addressed in what seemed like calligraphy. That note was from Ana Garibaldi. It read plainly: *I don't want you to be alone.*

TEN

It had been a long while since he'd cleaned up after himself—he had people for that. Perhaps it was because surgery was so exacting that he had no taste for it. Once outside the operating room he tended to let things go. His life was in this sense like Einstein's hair: the unkempt result of intense focus elsewhere.

But an orderly desk is an aid to a man with troubles, and this Gallin knew the way a lung knew to breathe. It was the same truth that fueled his practice, bought his bread and sumptuous butter: appearances count. Whether it came packaged as a neat desk, a manicured lawn, or fat-free eyelids, an orderly veneer promised a balanced interior—just as a grape's shape foretold its flavor.

Every appearance was really that: a promise. A promise to be as one seems. We were all projections, expressions, surfaces, faces. And so Gallin was straightening up. Getting it together.

On his desk a stack of soulless magazines had collapsed and widened, their glossy surfaces repellent and slippery even to one another. These he marshaled into architectural piles on the floor, flush at the corners. For the myriad patient files, fugitive from their tall black aluminum home in Janine's office, he made temporary residence in a printer paper box. The box, too, went to the floor. This was easy, satisfying. Why didn't he do it more often? Each item he touched seemed to correspond to some mental obstacle, and as he removed one he excised both.

This little bit of clearing gave Gallin a better view of the immediate landscape, and sundry objects now cried out for disposal. He was surprised by the ease with which he discarded phone messages and thank-you notes, untapped lifesavers and mint tins, notes to himself of faded importance and sixty-cent pens. He was a grim reaper of jetsam. Down into the copper can it went—domestic brush felled by his scythe-like hands—burying last Friday's tasteless but still astonishingly moist pickle, which at the beginning of this purgative sweep had lain alone on the can's stained bottom like a string tied to a finger for remembrance—a symbol of last week's life. In that life there was no Ana Garibaldi, Bernardo was grievously dead and Nick Adams was a disembodied voice on the telephone, someone to feel sorry for. Ancient history, personal pyramids. All that remained was his potential penury: he was still running out of money, his practice in peril. It was a circumstance he needed to address, but which was taking a beating on his list of priorities.

He threw more stuff away. Was he too about to start anew? Following Bernardo? First though, could he really do what Bernardo was asking? He realized solemnly that whatever his personal actions, the final chapter would read the same—Bernardo was gone, had already escaped, whether Gallin chose to comply or not. Still there was more to a story than how it ended. There was getting there. And in a serious way Gallin was already complicit. Knowledge made one just as complicit as action.

Next went the desiccated roses, last week's living pleasure. He palmed their slimy stems and stuffed the tops down into the can. A couple of petals escaped, seesawing down with languid indirectness to the floor, the weight of dreams. He ground these into the rug with the sole of his shoe. That's just what the Persians had done, he thought, made dye from flowers. Everything, even the rug, was a work in progress. Now he was adding to it. For that brief moment, with his heel raised and twisting, he wished he had become a dancer. What it would be to live through your body alone. He imagined the solitary work before the mirror, the rote repetition in the studio, late into the night, dancing against the fear of failure. He did not think of himself at that moment as a man crushing rose petals.

Vase in hand he walked to the small brass sink on the wall next to his favorite globe—a grapefruit-size sphere meticulously crafted by a Londoner in 1776. He spun it now, enjoying the marvelous monotony of hue it produced in revolution—most of the land and all the seas wearing the deep blue cloak of British imperium. Its portrayal of dominance was not accurate, not for the era anyway, but it showed the ambition.

This blue ball doubly delighted him because he was convinced its color derived from the legendary blue of Elizabeth I's conquering virgin eyes. The virgin queen was his consistent answer to the ribald cocktail party question about what personage from history one would most want to fuck, given the chance. Most doctors, he noticed, tended to say Cleopatra.

The rose stems had bled their green life into the water and he poured the kale-colored liquid onto the four loose breast implants he kept in the sink. These were the samples he sometimes pressed against women's breasts during consultations. With particularly small-breasted women he could often feel their hearts thump as they sat there boldly reimagining themselves. If their husbands or boyfriends came with them, Gallin liked to give the man a good-size implant to hold during the consult—350 ccs or so. Since he had started doing this he'd found amazing results: every woman whose husband played with an implant during the consult booked and had the surgery. Every single one. Who knew? It was quite a study. Even on rare occasions when he was not especially eager to win over a patient—call it intuition; being able to spot a future malcontent was part of the job—Gallin could almost never resist the urge to toss a saline pouch across his desk to the husband, watching the man's head bob excitedly, nervously, tracking the fluid gem's wobbly flight in order to stab it in the air. The men were always desperate not to miss it, determined not to send the message that a big new breast was something they couldn't handle.

There was little more powerful than holding what you wanted in your hands. Once a man held a new possibility, had juggled it and was given permission to imagine it, it was hard to let go.

The globe came to a graceful halt and Gallin's eyes set, as the sun famously never did, upon the British Empire. What a tiny place Britain was now, he considered. How the years disappeared into centuries. This century might be the worst yet. Look at the

103

last—we barely made it out and then what a start to this one. It seemed as if the world had spent all its love. Run out of it, like love was some kind of fossil fuel. He had brought a son into the world and now the son was leaving voluntarily. But then again Bernardo was not giving up on love, was he? He was in some way after it, no? Whatever faith Gallin managed still to hold onto lay somehow in the notion of love. Love was the only thing that ever made one feel bigger than one's circumstances. That fit with what Bernardo was doing. Hell, by that definition he was a giant: leaving a love-less world in search of something more.

His desk a model of order, he sat at it and spun around, logging on to the Internet. His password gave him a kick each time he entered it: ALEACH. That was Cary Grant's real name, Archie Leach. To Gallin there was no more perfect entrée to the cyber-world. In that place void of faces, where exaggeration of the iden-tity gap—the gulf between one and one's presented self—was expected, even encouraged, the power of Grant's invented per-sona invoked by the entry of the humble *ALeach*, it was sublime. The only problem with his password was his pride in it, for he could not stop revealing it to people! He loved telling what it was. Everyone agreed it was an inventive, smart, even a beautiful pass-word. ("Richard, it's *surpassing*," Donnie Theissen had said on Saturday night, before Gallin started throwing his darts around the party.) The password was so suitable for the task. "We all want to be Cary Grant," Leach had said. "Even I," he confessed, "want to be him."

Presently, Gallin badly needed a dose of the world outside his own head. For this he went to CNN.com, where assertive head-lines led to stories without much in the way of verifiable facts or interesting detail. This topic-only news style, which framed the world without painting it in, was useful if one had previous knowl-edge of the subject at hand. The style was smart, really, because the product—the news—obviously had to satisfy a lot of people with different levels of understanding. More and more people all the time, in fact, needed the news, as even people who didn't used to watch or read it now tuned in constantly to see what to be afraid of.

For Gallin the CNN style worked well—he could often supply a story with the significant details reporters either didn't know or didn't bother to reveal. Perhaps they thought it was of no interest if one country in a story purchased all its rice or oil or heroin or landmines from the other country being mentioned. But for Gallin this kind of detail was what made the stories sensible. He wondered what people who didn't know such details could possibly make of the news.

Nevertheless, CNN satisfied a certain shallow headline hunger in him. It was a quick fix, making him feel passably if loosely connected to the world. By giving him the daily topics, CNN seemed to promise at least that the world had not forgotten him. In the deal, he'd do the same for it.

He was on the third paragraph of a short fable comparing New York's crusading attorney general to Wyatt Earp when Bernardo said, softly, "Dad?" from the doorway.

The stillness of the voice, like something you hear after it's happened, startled him. He couldn't remember if Bernardo had always been so quiet, whether it was a trait of his. He thought perhaps it had been.

"Sit down, son," he said.

The command in his own voice surprised Gallin. It surprised him so much he thought his voice might say something on its own, without his consent. But Gallin's reaction was nothing compared to how such vocal assuredness affected Bernardo. His father's authority sounded to him like nectar. For months he had been on his own, seeking in the largest sense, trying to make impossible decisions with no one to consult. Suddenly to be told even the simplest thing declaratively, to be given an order, told to sit, was Edenic.

He followed the command, hoping for more.

"Bernardo, let's talk."

Gallin continued to hope his voice might proceed on its own. It disappointed.

"Okay," Bernardo said.

"You really feel that you understand, comprehend completely, what you're giving up?"

"I do. It's nothing that's not already gone, honestly."

"If you're certain about it then why do you want to see your son? Have you given that any more thought? Don't you think it's cruel? He's grown. He can't speak yet, but he could recognize you. You want to show yourself and take it away again? He's an innocent." Gallin spoke with wonderful calm. He would order the world by this contained vocal music. He continued: "The word that keeps coming into my mind is irrevocable. If you're already gone, as you say, then you wouldn't need to see him. It shows a crack in your armor, son. A crack in your plan."

"I'm not sure that's true, Dad. One thing I'm doing now is going with my instincts, instead of against them. I *feel* I want to see him. I feel that there's something I can communicate to him that he'll be able to keep even if he doesn't understand what it is. I have this idea that I can hold him, I don't know, sort of perfectly, and that he'll always feel it. Sounds crazy but I think it's real."

"It sounds no crazier than the rest of this."

In fact Gallin tended to believe in the sort of spiritual transmission Bernardo proposed. He believed in karma. That a father's touch could be imprinted on a son's heart to lasting effect gave him no trouble at all. What did trouble him was how outweighed such an act would be by the heavier act of sheer abandonment.

"Because to be honest," Bernardo continued, "I didn't have any love for him before. Now I don't want to leave him with that feeling. When I looked at him before, I felt anguish. A child—even an infant—must feel that. I think if I could just touch him now I could reverse it. Because I don't feel that way anymore. I want to try to reverse it so he doesn't feel that bad air in him all his life."

The notion was elegantly conceived, even beautiful. But only if you believed that Bernardo had discovered some higher truth, as he claimed. It worked only if you believed his actions were noble, in service of something larger. If you believed what he was doing was right. Gallin wanted to.

Bernardo's physical appearance did suggest that something transformative was happening. Again, since yesterday, he'd changed. His face had softened slightly, no longer quite the angular arrowhead, and his eyelashes seemed longer, thicker. It was strange: today with his simple plans and cold contingencies he resembled more a dull priest stirring an old fire than last night's hot bony risen Christ. Even his eyes, which had finally seemed to fit him, were different. They returned less light, soaking it in instead of reflecting it. Bernardo's eyes seemed to be devouring all they could of this world he was leaving. They were storing it, packing it away. Gallin had seen the same in dying eyes.

"Dad, I feel no guilt. At first I did. It was horrible, like being in a vice. It squeezed on my head, my gut, everywhere. It was the first time I felt pressure literally. But then things gradually got better. Then the world that pretends to need you goes forward without you. Then you read in the *New York Times* about how they've buried you, and then the guilt sort of just drops away. Melts into a sort of crystal you can use for strength."

"I'VE ALWAYS thought guilt was important. Part of the balances. One of the checks."

Gallin was caught in a thought: it would be helpful if his eyes did change—if the change he now noticed was the beginning of a metamorphosis in progress. These eyes—Christa's stolen diaphanous orbs—were too distinctive as they were: all the facial surgery in the world wouldn't keep them from giving him away. Still, it was a common mistake to think that eyes were immutable, like fingerprints. They weren't. Sometimes you had to laugh at the poets (diaphanous orbs!) but they got this much right: the eyes went with the soul.

"Besides," Gallin continued, "nobody buried you, Bernardo. We just had to move a little forward, or pretend to move, that's all."

"I don't blame anyone, Dad. I'm doing the same thing."

"Let me ask you this, then." Gallin felt his voice rise from deep inside him. "Isn't what you're doing cowardly? You talk as if you're pursuing some heroic path—this courageous reinvention, this brave steely-eyed recognition of different worlds. To a degree I understand that. But you realize you can't really start over." Gallin was unsure if this last was a question. "I mean, you don't have amnesia—you know who you are. This isn't some Harrison Ford movie. I can change your face and you can change your posture and even your outlook, I grant you, but your essential self? You can't do that. You can go work on some fishing boat off the coast of Oregon. You can go and do any of the million ideas you may have that supposedly constitute a simple life, a pure life. You can go and drive an ice cream truck if you want. But there is continuity to a life. A life accumulates. It builds—you can't truncate that, pick and choose. So what's so brave or great about the illusion that you can?"

"Pretend to be a thing all your life and at the end that's what you'll have been, right Dad?" It was an answer Bernardo had ready. His tone was sharp.

"*All* your life!" Gallin replied. "You're missing a key ingredient if that's your response. The ALL. You're missing the all."

"Dad, I don't think it's denial or illusion. I think it's a natural progression—a legitimate second stage of my particular life that I have to try. God, the way it happened is almost supernatural. When I say I have to, I mean I have to," his tone bent down again, respectful. There was a quiet radiance in it. He had thought things through. Even when you were wrong there was grace in having thought things through.

"One man's cowardice, another man's bravery, is that it? And is anybody—is either man right?" Gallin wanted an answer but knew if there was one it, too, was in the future. With the other answers. He was resigned to that. He had the question, at least. "Well just tell me what happened then. They found your wedding ring in the rubble—"

"I threw it. I don't know why. Just my first reaction to the second plane. I was waiting after the first one. Strange, huh? Not running, just waiting. My memory of it is a little mixed up. But what I remember thinking was: what's next? There must be more.

108

There's another scene, I know it. I had a weird feeling it wasn't over. Even after the second one I thought it would go on for days and days, or years. I thought the Empire State was next, and the Golden Gate Bridge—"

"Didn't you think to call me or call your wife and say 'I'm okay.' You know you can divorce your wife and move to goddamn Oregon without a bunch of plastic surgery and this secretive crap."

The soothing voice gave way; the rough man had crashed breathless through the smooth surface of his tone. Gallin was angry, but perplexed by his anger: it was mixed up so thoroughly with admiration that he didn't know if the anger was toward Bernardo or himself. What had the boy done, other than what he and his country had for a lifetime instructed him to do? To take control of his life. We pounded it into them, the children. We said anyone who didn't take control was still a child. You can be anything you want, we said. All you need is the desire. We said it to kids in the projects and in the barrio and at Andover and at the schools for the blind. You make your bed, you lie in it, we cautioned. No wonder everybody went crazy—who really made his own bed? It didn't work that way, did it? But Bernardo was trying. Yet his plan was so presumptuous, so enormous. He was attempting to assume a level of control over his life—his destiny— that was so rare. No one had as much control as this. Gallin didn't know if it could be achieved. It was too fantastic. Time was still beyond our control. It made him think of Icarus. What was Icarus anyway, a hero or a fool? Was it a tragedy, that story? What was the lesson they used Icarus to teach?

"I did think to call," Bernardo replied. "I did. I wanted to. But then I was walking and walking—the smoke and the soot were just incredible—and I don't know, I just didn't. And after a few days I started to know I wouldn't. I really can't explain it fully."

"How about a little bit more then. Can you explain it a little bit more? That's not too much to ask, is it?"

Bernardo shifted in his chair.

"It won't make any sense to you or anyone else, Dad. I know that. That's something I have to live with. There's no one thing that caused me to do what I did—or what I'm doing. It's not simple like that," he paused and took a deep breath. "All of a sudden I felt like I would be calling across some uncrossable boundary. To a different world, an old world. Like it was a time trick and I'd been pushed into my future. It was clear to me that I wasn't supposed to contact the past, that the past was an untouchable place I could infect somehow by touching, like the atmosphere wouldn't support me and that if I reached across the divide it would be wrong. I know this sounds crazy, but I had seen the other side of things somehow and to go back would be bad for both sides."

"But none of that is true, Bernardo. You weren't in the future. It's not actual, what you felt, it's—"

"But Dad it's truly what I felt, still feel. What's to say that it's not actual. If you don't at some point in life go with your gut, with what you feel, then what good is having a gut? I mean you have a gut for a reason, I have to figure. Right? And the reason can't be to ignore it all the time."

"But why not—even if your gut is telling you to change your life—why not do it the simpler way, the cleaner straighter way? Get a divorce, move to Alaska, sell hot dogs, I don't know, whatever you need to do. But why cause all this pain? Why make people suffer?"

"You think there's more pain this way? I don't think so, Dad."

"Yes, I think you've caused an enormous amount of pain. I know it has, for me personally. I lived it and witnessed your wife and others go through it—not to mention that it's criminal. And you've caused me some serious problems in that regard too."

"Look, this way I don't abandon my son, my wife is never walked out on, they're rich from the settlement. It doesn't look like my choice but it actually is. This is as clean as it gets."

"You were rich anyway."

"No, not like this. I was overextended. You of all people should know what I'm talking about." Bernardo threw a quick, comprehensive glance around the lush office, indicating his father's own extensions. At least, Gallin thought, he had never hid much from

110

his son: Bernardo knew the way he lived. "This way they're set. And I'm free and where I'm supposed to be. The other way we get neither of those."

He stopped abruptly, having just registered what Gallin had said a moment ago. He scrunched his brow, previewing wrinkles that would one day set in deeply, no matter his will.

"What do you mean 'serious problems'?" Bernardo asked.

"I've got a guy on my ass trying to extort money from me—and now he leaves me a note that says he saw you."

"No."

"Yes."

"Fuck. Who is he?"

"He's nobody—a third-rate journalist from what I can tell. I think he reviews music for *New York* magazine. You know who he is? You remember Peter, my nurse—it's his disgruntled lover."

"You think it's a real problem?"

"Not if you're gonna go to Oregon with a new face it's not. But you realize if I do this and you get caught, I'm complicit in massive insurance fraud and I'm sure a shitload of other crimes as well."

"Dad, the plan is for me to get out. That's it. Out. I've got new papers, pretty legit, should be able to set myself up no problem. You give me life again."

Gallin wanted to think this was true. "New papers?" he asked.

"Birth certificate, Florida driver's license. A bank account in the new name. Not very difficult, very authentic."

"What is it?"

"What?"

"The new name."

"You don't want to know and I don't want you to know. After this Dad, it's a real goodbye."

"Oh that's okay," Gallin said, sarcasm creeping in. "I'm accustomed to saying goodbye now. By the way, will you be coming back again? When will you change your mind?"

"You know I can't change my mind. And the surgery insures it. By the way, I don't think this is heroic, just necessary. I guess I do hope there's something brave about realizing that. You want to know what I was doing at work that morning?"

"Listen," Gallin said, "here's what I'm thinking, and there's a very large problem with it, so listen carefully to me. We can do this surgery Wednesday night, but I need a nurse. The only person I can think of to come at that hour is Peter—he's also the only one I can trust from a competence standpoint. But I don't know how far we can trust him for discretion, and especially with this nutcase he's living with. But I can't do it without a nurse."

"So what do we do?"

"I'm thinking about going down to talk to him, feel him out. He may not even know what his boyfriend is up to. In fact, I bet he doesn't. I figure I'm going to have to offer him decent money—we should give him ten thousand for the night."

"All right, I can take care of that. No problem."

"But then you have to understand there's always someone who will know. Someone besides us. I can't tell whether that's going to be a problem down the road or not. Usually, if you can't tell, it is."

"Is there anybody else you can use?"

"No. A ten PM surgery will raise suspicions—I can't just hire freelance for that. That'll assure chatter. It's not a big community."

"Okay, it's Peter then. I can leave you another ten thou in case he needs it later, to keep quiet. That's a lot of money to him, right?"

"I would think. Still, I don't like the risk. Not so much him—I think he'll be okay. But this Nick Adams, his partner, I don't like him near this. It scares me, though I don't think people will necessarily see him as credible. Besides, by definition this story is unbelievable—he'll sound like a kook trying to get it heard."

"You think?"

"Well, yes. If it weren't happening to you, would you believe it? Plus the guy is a little *off*, strange. I'll keep thinking about it, but right now I don't see another way."

"Well, let me know what I can do," Bernardo said as casually as if he were volunteering to help out at a party. "Dad, thank you. I know you don't believe in this. That makes it mean even more to me. You always sort of went with your gut, didn't you?" The question was rhetorical.

"Sorry," Bernardo continued, "I have to press you further. I'm sorry, I am: Will you help me to see Tyler, Dad, just for five minutes, just for a minute?"

"I'll see if I can bring him over tomorrow morning. No promises. And I'll tell you again I don't think you should see him. I think it's going too far."

"I know. I understand. But wouldn't you want to see your son?" At that moment, in that context, it was the strangest question Gallin had ever been asked. He had no answer.

"So what were you doing—at work that day?"

"Oh, yes. Brutal. Do you know where Chennai is?"

"In the south of India?"

"Right. Well, they've got a very highly educated population there—you know, strong caste system, proud people. Of course, they've got nothing to do with their education once they get it because there's no economy there. Anyway, a couple of years ago these two Princeton guys, my age, raise a bunch of money and go down there and start this company called TigerServices and start selling every service you can imagine to the big banks and everyone else. Starts out with simple stuff, building PowerPoint presentations and copyediting, and in a year they're doing serious market analysis for, like, fifteen bucks an hour. So Bentley wants in. Our heavy hitters had turned down the Princeton guys when they had the chance. Too risky. And now they're pissed."

"Of course."

"So we find two Harvard guys to basically do the same damn thing, mirror the operation, call it CrimsonServiceStar. Not very original, but you don't need to reinvent the wheel, right? Anyway, it turns out we need to bring in more Indians on the ownership side because some of the bigwig locals feel locked out of the profits from the Tiger operation. We say fine, fine, bring in the local partners, just to placate the natives and not get tied up in the bureaucracy, which can be on the slow side. Actually, in India, the bureaucracy can more or less strangle a business to death if

113

it wants to, like a python. It's no coincidence that it's the land of snake charmers. So these local chiefs we cut in are going to help push our agenda through—maybe even give us an edge over the Tigers. What we don't know is that our guys have an ugly business on the side that they divert a good chunk of our funds to."

"Kidneys?" Gallin asked.

"Yes! How did you know that? It turns out some of our money to train locals was funding the world's largest kidney transplant hub. Totally unsafe, unregulated, people dying. Basically just poor people with no options left selling their kidneys on the black market. Doctors—supposed doctors—leaving people to die a quarter of the time, shipping the kidneys all over the world, lots to the U.S, using our money."

"I had a friend in medical school who spent some time there years back. It's been that way for a while, a hotbed for kidneys."

"But our money—the money I approved for Bentley—turned the existing kidney business into a big-time global operation. We were killing people."

"So you were pulling out the money?"

"No. Honestly, I was just thinking about the situation, not doing anything. We were already in it, you know?"

ELEVEN

That night the weather hollowed into a bracing windless freeze that stung his face and Gallin, heavily scarved and gloved but hatless lit out in the dark toward one of his city beacons, retracing his steps from earlier, up to the top of the park and then west, wanting to swallow with his eyes the great gothic extravagance of St. John the Divine, where he was married thirty-three years before and where he married his son, too, in tiny mimicry of the original; he wants to stand on its stone stairs and ask its incredible unfinished façade to validate him, and he does, he stands there in the quiescence, an ambulance on its way to St. Luke's just once breaking through with a chirped burp of siren and flashed red fright, standing until he'd let enough snot run down his nose and from wiping coated his good gloves with a mucus mother-of-pearl and he listened for the sky to speak—to say something profound or utter some low, transcendent tone that he could translate in his favor—while he paced under the friezes of the saints asking if he really deserved what was on his hands now, whether it is ever the case that we get what we deserve when suddenly he developed an acute hunger, so powerful that for the first time he believed he knew what starvation was, what so many in the world had daily to bear, and he thought that it was the sky sending him this obscure answer to his question, this empathetic hunger sent so he could know it and become more truly human, his earthly experience deeper, greater, wider, meaner, and with this revelation came at once the need to sate it, a need that shivered in him as he bounded down the stairs for Amsterdam and southward toward the bright deli sign at 109th Street, moving toward that jumpy neon as if it said salvation rather than sandwiches, and

115

getting almost to it, just to the corner when he felt the sting of the blade enter just below his hip and realized there were four of them and he was suddenly not on Amsterdam, but ten feet from the corner, on 109th now, then fifteen feet moving on his own but being helped too, to the stoop, the avenue seeming a mile away, like a beach from shallow surf that hides a riptide, and the pain shot down his leg like lightning and up into his burning stomach as he realized that they had chosen him, targeted him, and then had taken him and that he was a long way if only a couple of miles from home.

The four were close up on him, surrounding him on the stoop. But it was quickly apparent there was no consensus among them about the proceedings. For a moment, they seemed to forget Gallin altogether.

"You were supposed to just scare him, bitch," said a nervous voice. "Stupid shit. Scare the fucker and he give it up. Why you go cuttin'?"

"Scare, scare, scare, nigger," replied another. This voice was ferocious. "That's all the shit you talk—scare 'em. No tienes pelotas. You gotta *get* shit, nigger. We ain't playin' no *ghost* shit—goin' boo and shit. You gotta *take*. You gotta hurt to take."

A third voice chuckled. "Dis nigga's crazy," he said and pushed the one who had just spoken. He pushed him playfully, with affection—he was having a good time. "He serious, yo. What I'm talkin' about. Nigga crazy *and* serious."

Sitting on the stoop, Gallin kept his head down, trying to get his bearings. Their shadows, tall and lean or short and thick, depending on their correlation to the light, moved flatly on the sidewalk at his feet, their voices clear but visages vague, like in a radio thriller.

The sidewalk was dingy with excretions: dark stripes of grease, gummy tar spots. Clumps of human hair hid under a curbside tire, swept out from a beauty parlor on Amsterdam and left to roll in the wind. An airborne grime clung like a scab to the streetlamps, mugging the light. The scene he watched now in shadows was black, dark—a scene from a larger tragedy, the urban street. He was miscast there, he thought.

Gallin's wound was small and clean. There had been no twisting of the knife—only the jab of the blade and its lightning reversal, a tongue forsaking a promise.

Staring at these dark shapes, gesticulating on the floor of New York—the world momentarily reduced to two dimensions—Gallin felt a discordant jolt of hope. He hoped the worst was past, here and elsewhere. Doubling over the flannel of his trousers he pressed hard with the heel of his hand to staunch the bleeding. He drew his feet back beneath his knees to try to hide them: his new sneakers glowed embarrassingly white. Somehow he wanted to fit in, be dressed right for this, on the side of power. The simplicity of his sneakers broadcast his obsolescence. Leather flags, they were, flying the blank alabaster of his desuetude.

On their feet, all he dared look at, he recognized four baroque variations on the moonshoes that had so perplexed him in the Foot Locker the week before. But what perplexed him now was how the wide frayed cuffs of their black jeans dragged along the ground, purposely ruined, even obscuring the majority of their magnificent shoes like parachutes draped over space capsules. What kind of style was this—this calculated ruination? Gallin did not want to be the captive of boys who cared so little as to let their pants drag on the ground.

Help might come. But the street seemed deserted.

"Pops, yo pops. Quit fuckin' around. You ain't hurt. That shit don't hurt. Cash and that watch and we walk away. Simple shit."

Gallin switched hands to keep pressure on the bleeding and held out his left arm, surrendering the watch. It was worth four-thousand dollars and, of course, nothing.

Taking a chance, he looked up. His persecutors stood above him shod identically in black nylon-shelled jackets. They wore black plastic sunglasses and NBA hats. Gallin recognized the Heat, the 76ers.

"'Kay now, cash," the stabber agitated. "Bitch, you better have Benjamins too—don't fuck around. I ain't bladin' nobody for some shit twenties." He pulled Gallin forward and yanked his wallet from his back pocket. In it were four hundreds and a ten. "Damn, bitch. Nice. You got some more? C'mon, what's in your pockets?"

Gallin reached with his right hand into his front pocket, producing another forty dollars. He held it out in his hand and the 76er, the jocular one, took it.

"You goddamn picked a good one. Shit," he said. "You crazy, but you a good picker bitch." He laughed. Then he said: "You see our pets?" Gallin, whose head was again down, traced the long shadow of the boy's hand along the ground. It pointed at a row of gray plastic garbage cans that lined the front of the building. Between the cans a frenetic army of brown rats was attacking a pigeon corpse. "That's our pets, motherfucker. That's *our* street. You like 'em? You wanna eat one?"

Suddenly there was a voice behind them. "Cut the shit," it said quietly. "Yo-I-said cut the shit."

They all turned.

"The fuck you doin'?" He got closer. "Serious—what the fuck's the problem? This my building. You forget or somethin'? Trouble here means trouble, dumb fucks."

"Ah Mig, we jus' had to take this one," said the stabber, sounding half-contrite. "C'mon look at him, just set up to be took."

"Cops come round here looking in about this and it's my dime, dumb fucks. Trouble where there ain't any now. What'd you get? Let me see?"

"Benjis baby!" said the stabber. "And the real time, yo."

He dangled Gallin's watch from his finger.

"Gimme that," said the newcomer, snatching the watch.

Gallin took a chance.

"I need to go to a doctor," he said, staring at the ground. "I don't have anything else. I won't say what happened."

"Shut up," the stabber said.

"I'll keep the watch," said the newcomer. "You keep the green and get the fuck gone. I'll take care of this." Gallin could sense the newcomer's authority. He wanted to trust it.

The stabber started to object, calling for justice—the watch was his, goddamn it. But his pleas were smote by the new one, who got right up in his face and said simply, "Don't," with cancerous severity. That ended it. They dispersed, half-laughing. Gallin and the new one were alone.

"Yo, old school, your shiny new whites walked you too far didn't they?"

He sat down on the stoop next to Gallin. "Cold as shit out here," he said. "What're you doin' up here? Shit-I-mean besides gettin' robbed?"

Gallin was terrifyingly confused—he was starving, bleeding, freezing, yet he felt saved, too. Was it a trick? It could be a trick, he thought. They could be working together. Where in the world was he?

"You remember me, old school?" Gallin didn't look up. "C'mon man, I sold you them shoes. Look," he said, grabbing Gallin's face and turning it toward him. Ana leapt into Gallin's mind. Two people in two days now had touched his face. So rare: Andrea almost never touched his face. No one did. Yet he touched faces all the time. In his life he must have touched thirty thousand faces.

Now he stared into the eyes of his savior. He saw the white scar and recognized it, sliding down from ear to lip like a narrow mountain range on a globe. It was the boy from the Foot Locker, in the referee uniform—the one who castrated Air Jordan with a box cutter. Replaying the last few minutes in his mind, he recalled one of the others referring to him as Mig. Gallin remembered the name tag he wore: Miguel. He couldn't believe he remembered. The fact that he could remember made him feel safe.

"I do. I do remember," he said. "You give very good service."

It was an idiotic thing to say.

"Ha," Miguel laughed. "You're funny, old school."

Gallin found himself following Miguel inside the building, down a narrow corridor with urine yellow walls painted over so many times they bulged unevenly, giving a feeling of vertigo. The floor was covered by small white tiles, most of which were cracked or loose. It was streaked with mud, dragged-in dog shit maybe. To his relief Gallin found it was not more painful to walk than to sit immobile—that the sharp pain was giving way to a dull throb. He was lucky: the knife could have clipped a ligament or muscle, but it had hit the corporeal equivalent of air.

In front of him Miguel's broad shoulders ascended the stairs purposefully, with a soldier's sturdy ease. He was short-framed but his powerful legs were ideally proportioned for the climb, which he executed lightly like a march, lending the grim corridor dignity. What was he doing? Gallin asked himself. But the boy had said he'd help him—and though Gallin thought for a moment that he should run, that he should try to get away, the escape impulse was quickly crushed by a nervous litany of reason. The boy, after all, had helped him. And now he walked in front of Gallin, hardly the position of a captor. Obviously he meant him no harm. What if he did try to flee? What then? He couldn't run, not on his riddled leg, benign as the wound was. And another thing: where were the four who'd attacked him? Laying in wait? Angry he'd been rescued from them? He had no choice but to follow. The stairs creaked loudly under Gallin's awkward gait, though Miguel trod them hardly causing a sound.

At the third floor, Gallin trailed Miguel into an apartment in the back of the building, hot as a cauterizer, and small. The room they entered was both kitchen and living area—the former section piled high with canned food and fruit. In the living area, on a worn-out couch, a large twelve-year-old boy, layered with fat, sat watching a huge late-model television with the sound off, eating peanut butter out of the jar with a spoon. He changed the channels steadily as if in a trance. On either side of the boy were curled up two little girls, neither more than three years old, half asleep despite the efforts of the screen to captivate them. One fought a freight train of yawns. The fat boy nodded when Miguel and Gallin entered, saying nothing. If he was surprised by the intrusion of a tall white bleeding doctor, it would have taken a polygraph to tell.

The only light in the place glowed from the TV, while the heat seemed to press in from everywhere. But the TV light was enough for Gallin to survey the room, which all told was perhaps ten by twenty. There looked to be two rooms in the back, too, each half the size of this one. Bedrooms, he assumed. The kitchen, despite being crowded with groceries, was immaculate. Only the refrigerator, covered with photographs and tattered crayon drawings, looked disorderly.

"Come here," Miguel said to Gallin, pulling out a chair from beneath the small round table stuffed against the wall. "Sit," he said. Then looking over Gallin's shoulder he said, "Yo, Sweets, take the girls across now to Theresa's, okay?"

In a sad war with his excess, the fat boy rumbled himself up, and grabbed the girls in one hand each as if they were baby birds. Outside, Gallin could hear the guttural insistence of pigeons. More than the stacked cans of soup and beans, the mango and eggplant, or enormous bags of chips and rice arranged tidily along the counter, it was the sound of the pigeons that reminded him of his hunger. He could not remember having eaten for days.

The fat boy squeezed through the door with the girls, nodding passively, still silent. It closed behind him with a bang. The TV flickered on. Walt Frazier with his Elvis sideburns was talking into a microphone, standing at half-court in Madison Square Garden.

"That's my brother, Sweets," Miguel said, indicating the door with his hand. "He likes candy."

"I understand," replied Gallin, not understanding his own reply.

"You bleedin' out?" Miguel asked, wetting a towel at the sink and handing it to Gallin.

"Thank you," Gallin said. He took the towel and pressed it against his pants. "It's not bad I don't think. I'll have to look at it."

"Go ahead," Miguel said, tugging on the end of his belt.

Gallin stood and unbuckled his belt, guiding his pants down to his knees. He sat down again as if on the toilet and dabbed the cut directly with the towel.

"No, it's not bad," Gallin reported. "Lucky. Just a couple of stitches. It'll be just like a deep bruise. Only a couple inches from the femoral artery. Listen, thank you."

"It's all right, dog. I like you. You're cool. We were trying to fuck with you a little in the store but you were cool," he said. "You like your old school kicks there, old school?" he asked, pointing to Gallin's bright white shoes. In here too Gallin was embarrassed by them.

"I do. Thank you again. They are good shoes. I've been walking twice today—*unfortunately.*"

Gallin was trying to remember more about Miguel from the store on Friday, but all he could summon was a sensation of fear. There was something jagged about him, like a broken bottle. He recalled more vividly the way the boys had talked, with that stigmatic energy that had so impressed him, and then the knife throwing. Looking now in the uneven light, Gallin was convinced there was a drastic change in his host's appearance, even since Friday, but he couldn't place it. Then he noticed the holes in his face.

"Yeah, they don't know shit what they're doin'. Stupid Dominican niggers and the dumb Puerto Rican that cut you. They never been nowhere, seen nothing. So they got blades out on the street when there ain't no call for blades. They act bad, think they're strong but they're soft. I could have those stupid fucks work for me but I don't want 'em."

"At the store?" Gallin asked, confused.

"Nah, man, work for me out there. In the street. Those little fucks can't play no straight game, workin' in no store. Not at all. Too stupid."

A bright car commercial came on. A convertible drove along the Pacific Coast Highway late in the afternoon, chasing the sun along the cliffs. The light from the screen illuminated Miguel's face. He'd had those rings in his lips and through his nose, Gallin remembered. They were gone. The holes they left were serious.

Attending his leg, Gallin asked: "Do you have any thin thread, or dental floss?"

"Maybe. You know what you're doin'?"

"I think so, yes."

Miguel walked into a bathroom without closing the door. He started rummaging in a mirrored cabinet. He barely fit in the room. The bathroom too, Gallin could see, was extremely clean. It sparkled. Miguel spoke while he looked, his back to Gallin for the second time.

"The DR and PR little boys ain't seen shit. You know where I'm from?" he asked, not waiting for a reply. "Nicaragua, man. We seen some shit in Nicaragua."

Gallin figured he could give this five or six stitches, which would hold it until he could get home. Miguel continued, bent down now looking under the sink.

"My father was a soldier in the army against the fucking Sandinistas. He was a colonel in the rebel army. You call them Contras. He was a colonel. Until I was fifteen we lived in an army camp in the hills."

Miguel emerged empty-handed from the tiny bathroom and opened a cluttered kitchen drawer to continue searching.

"We came here nine years ago with my mama when I was fifteen, almost sixteen. She's educated, Mama. She went to university in Managua. She was a poet and she was supposed to teach here at Columbia University. I thought when we left Nicaragua we were going to the country, to Colombia the country. But we came here—to Columbia the university. We were supposed to have special privileges because of my father, from being with the Americans. But she taught for just the first summer we're here and then there is no more teaching and she has to clean houses. She should never have been in love with my father, but she was in love with him totally because he was so brave, she said. She was rich. When she was a girl she had diamonds. My father sold them to buy guns. Here you can have diamonds. There, what can you do with a diamond?"

Gallin wondered why he was hearing about this. He was attentive.

"My grandparents were rich people who lived in Managua in a house with walls around it. That's where Mama was a girl. But I never met them. After she married Papa they never talked to her again. Papa was poor, but he was a Catholic and he could speak English. He was trained by the Americans."

Miguel found a spool of black glossy thread with a needle slipped through it. He held it up: "This?"

"Please, yes," Gallin replied. He took it. "Thank you. Can we boil some water?" he asked. "Just a bit?"

Miguel put a kettle on the gas stove. He turned the knob and it clicked loudly a half dozen times. A circle of flame erupted under the kettle. He turned it down.

"It's warm in here," Gallin offered by way of conversation. Seeing the flame made him feel even hotter.

"They like it," he nodded at an absent family. "Like home. And it is the only free thing in New York, the heat. It comes with the rent." The radiator, as if on cue, clanged and hissed. Miguel laughed. "In Nicaragua that is the sound of the people." He laughed again.

"When I was fourteen I became a soldier like my father—for two years before we came here in 1992. I was under my father's command. He was in charge of the whole camp. I learned English from the Americans too. I was in a special class that learned from the American in charge—his name was Gas House. It was only a nickname. Because of that I can speak better English than I do. If I want."

Gallin remembered how adeptly Miguel had switched dialects in the store, from street thug to voiceover. *How can I help you, sir*, he'd asked. Like Olivier, he'd sounded.

"Gas House trained my father and the regular soldiers to use the new guns and other weapons he brought in—like rocket launchers, and to use the walkie-talkies. Rocket launchers are the shit, man. Anyway, Gas House didn't look scary—he looked a little bit like you. But Papa said he was a "killer supreme." That's what he called him—*supremo*. Anyway, my father was a warrior. He died in battle. He was shot in the heart and they cut off his hands and his feet and left them next to his body. But everybody knows he gave them no satisfaction. He was too brave to give them satisfaction. That's why they didn't cut off his head, out of respect. Because he wouldn't let his men see him giving satisfaction. He taught us to be brave."

The kettle whistled. Gallin made a move to get it, but Miguel held up a hand for him to stay put. He put the kettle on a plate in front of Gallin and put a porcelain mug beside it. The mug bore the bright blue Columbia University crest. Gallin filled the mug and dropped the needle in. "Alcohol?" he asked hopefully.

"You gonna sew it up yourself, old school? You should go to a doctor."

"I am a doctor," Gallin replied.

"No shit. Serious? That's good—you can just fix yourself up. Wow, that is good. With regular thread."

"I'll re-suture it when I get home. If I get home. This will just stop the bleeding," he said. "Do you have any kind of alcohol?" he ventured again.

"Across the hall at my sister's. Hold on. She likes vodka. That okay?"

"That will do very well, yes. Thank you."

"You talk a little bit like Gas House too. Be right back."

Miguel disappeared out the door and was back in a minute. While he was gone Gallin sat with his eyes closed.

Miguel was talking as he came through the door.

"When I say he taught us to be brave, I mean the real shit. That's what I mean about the guys that took you out. They're so soft, livin' here. They seen nothin'. When I first went in—in the army, when I was fourteen—one of the things they do, my father did—was bury you. They bury you alive. It's supposed to test you. So you already know what it feels like to die, and so you never panic and give anybody any satisfaction that way. Buried alive, man. With me it was a special case too. My father buried me alive for four hours. With others it was only a few minutes, or maybe half an hour, but I was under for four hours. In a box three feet underground. You never heard a sound in your life like the sound of dirt shoveling on you. It's loud at first like thunder and then it gets real quiet, dull. Then you can hardly hear it, everything is muffled. You can't tell if they're still shoveling it on you or if they're just walking around up there, doing their business. Walking on top of you. For me it was eight o'clock in the morning

125

when they buried me, so I could hear sounds the whole time. When a gun fired it sounded the same like if you were scratching your ear.

"The colonel said I had to be down under the dirt longer than everybody else because it was easier for me. The other guys, he said, didn't know if someone was gonna dig them up or not. They thought they would get dug up but they couldn't be sure because it wasn't their papa in charge. He said since he was my father I was sure I was gonna get dug up—so I had to stay down longer. To have the same test. I was under for four hours. Buried alive for four hours. So now no matter what happens I'm not scared, you know? I can't be scared."

Gallin was without words.

"So I could get these pussies to work for me on the street. They're all scared shit of me because of that, and because they know I ain't scared, and because they know I killed people in real war. But I'm trying not to get stuck on the street. I seen people go down. I just want to do my little business out there, keep it so I can provide. I got Mama to help out and Sweets and my two sisters with the babies. My one sister married to a stupid ass Dominican who spends all his money pimpin' out his Honda. My other one just got the kids, no man."

Miguel stood up, took the mug and poured the hot water from it into the sink. He dumped the needle from the cup onto the plate.

"That good?" he asked.

"Yes, thank you. Thank you very much. Your name is Miguel right?"

"Yeah. That's good, old school. You got a good memory. What's yours?"

"Gallin. Dr. Richard Gallin."

"I'm named for the saint. You know about him?"

"Very little. The archangel?"

"You know a lot, old school. Yeah, he was a warrior. I was named for him because he was a warrior and so am I. He was a colonel, like my father, when God went to war with the Devil. Far

126

as I can tell that battle's still on. We studied it in school. My father was a Catholic, not an Indian. His people came from Spain. Lots of people think the rebels were all dirty Indians."

Gallin poured some vodka on the towel and pressed it on the cut. He began to suture with the black thread.

"What kind of doctor are you?"

"I'm a plastic surgeon."

"No shit?"

"No shit," Gallin replied.

"Get the fuck out of here," Miguel half laughed.

"I would like to very much, to tell the truth," Gallin said.

"You're funny, doc," Miguel replied. Gallin thought this sounded threatening. He did not like the idea of leaving being funny.

"Nah, I was just thinking—you think you could—you think maybe you could fix my face? Look at it?"

Gallin was finishing off his suture, tying off.

"I noticed you removed all those piercings."

Miguel put his face closer to Gallin's.

"I got the holes from that and this scar," he said, pointing to it.

Gallin stood up, pulled his pants back on. He felt a twinge of his earlier hunger, but looking at Miguel's face it vanished. He had a surgeon's strong stomach and little in the way of physical deformity bothered him, but he found self-mutilation repulsive. The holes the boy had punctured in his own face caught him up. He swallowed it down.

"You hungry?" Miguel asked.

"I am, in fact. Very."

"You like black beans?"

"I do, yes."

Stitched up now, Gallin was anxious for this to be over. His mind started to wander beyond this predicament to his others.

"Yesterday was shopping day. We get food for the month," he indicated the cans, the rice, the fruit. "Cabinets are filled too. We got it to spare early on."

He reached for a can of black beans. The picture on the label looked delicious to Gallin.

"Let me explain the deal right?" Miguel began again. "The reason I deal anything on the street is because that shit straight job at Foot Locker don't pay. I work all day in there and make forty-six bucks. All goddamn day. I only got that goin' so Mama feels better knowin' I got a straight job. Any straight job. A uniform makes it even better. But I make a week's pay in one hour on the street right? But I sort of like the straight job—that kind of life. Helpin' people like you is all right. Except it don't pay. If it paid right I'd never go on the street. On the street you gotta deal with shit like the stupid assholes that grabbed you.

"Plus I'm starting to think I want to be more American, I don't know. I'm flying my flag, you know, out my window. I mean Americans taught my father and they trained me before I even came here. But then I came here—to *America*—and it was supposed to be all great and it sucked you know? I was pissed. Mama gotta clean houses when she was supposed to teach at Columbia University. But since they knocked down the Twin Towers, I think different. I'm thinking being American all the way is the deal. It's not like I'm going back to Nicaragua. But my face got these holes from when I was pissed off and from even before that, before I came here. It's real hard to be American if people don't like your face. You think you can fix my face?"

He removed the bowl of beans from the microwave and poured hot pepper sauce in generously. He stuck a spoon in it and put it in front of Gallin. It smelled like a gourmet feast. Then he poured some vodka in the mug and pushed that toward Gallin too.

"Thank you," Gallin said. He ate ravenously and drank the vodka, which made him feel a little drunk.

When he finished he said, "Turn on the light. Let me see the scar a little better."

The ceiling light burst bright over the room and Miguel sat again in the chair across from Gallin, thrusting his face forward. Gallin noticed for the second time the optimistic beige eyes of the boy, the maternal love he detected in them originally so obviously manifest now, proven. Gallin ran his pinky finger softly along the scar, a keloid. Another face touched. And there were pockmarks

128

in his cheeks. It was true he looked dangerous. The boy stared at him, patient, hopeful.

"How did you get this?" Gallin asked about the scar.

"My father."

Gallin could not imagine any scene to explain this answer that was not heartbreaking.

"How old is it?" he asked.

"I was nine," he answered.

"Okay," Gallin said, feeling along the scar's ridge with his index finger. He pressed, trying to gauge the hardness of the deposit.

"The piercings," he continued, "how long did you have them?"

"Only two years," Miguel said brightly, proudly. He seemed to get younger as they spoke. "I just took them out yesterday."

"Okay," Gallin said, looking closely now under his lip at the four holes there, glancing only briefly at the hole in his nostril. Gallin took his hand away. He leaned back in his chair.

"I have a plan, doc. You're the missing piece. I wanna get my face fixed so I can get further in the white world. So I don't scare everybody so much. Once you know you're scarin' people you have to use it, cause you're scarin' 'em anyway. But if you're not, then you don't have to play scary. Know what I mean? Then I'm gonna go out one more time and make a big play. One big play, like ten-thou. Then I'm gonna go straight into the white world, with a new face and some money. Couple of nice suits. Totally American.

"It's like before we were only half-American. Even though I'm a citizen, it was like I wasn't really an American. But now everybody who's American is straight-up American you know? Because of the Twin Towers. Now if you're American—even if you're latino or nigger or whatever, as long as you ain't Taliban or some shit, you're cool. It's like they sent out new invitations to join up with America. Like they realized we're not the enemy. We don't wanna be attacked neither. So you can be American a hundred percent now. Almost totally. As long as you're not the enemy."

129

Gallin pointed hesitantly to the vodka and Miguel quickly poured him a little more. Gallin's mind was shuffling an idea he did not want to deal.

"You think you can fix my face, doc? Maybe for me saving your ass? On a trade sort of? You work on trade-offs ever?"

Gallin looked around the tiny apartment, a quarter the size of his office alone. It was home to an entire family. Did he work on trade-offs? In a sense, he did little else.

"Oh, and here's your watch, dog," Miguel said, pulling the watch from his pocket and returning it.

"Thank you."

"Seriously, how about that? Work on a trade-off. I even give you your watch back."

Gallin leaned back in his chair, stared up directly into the light.

"I will work on your face," he said. "It won't look better all at once, but it will eventually be much better."

Miguel beamed. He looked for an instant like a young boy, perhaps the boy he was at eight, before this scar.

"Serious? You really gonna help me like that?"

"I am."

"Shit, doc. I knew I liked you. From as soon as you walked in the store."

"Thank you." It was another odd reply, but it surprised him less.

He drank down the warm vodka in a short gulp. It burned the back of his throat. He took a deep breath through his mouth to cool it down. He was going to say it.

"And I have a proposition for you, beyond that," Gallin began. He looked at the boy, who was no longer beaming, no longer young again, but fierce-looking and focused.

"I will also pay you the ten-thousand dollars you want for your fresh start. I'll give you that money in cash, in addition to your face. But I want you to do something for me first."

"Anything," Miguel replied. It was the grim, powerful *anything* of a soldier.

"I want you to get somebody off my back," Gallin said, knowing at that moment that he had transgressed beyond where he could have ever imagined. "There is a man who is threatening me, trying to extort me, threatening my livelihood, my life. I need it taken care of."

"Where is he—is all I need to know," Miguel said in a tone that terrified Gallin. "That's all I need to know and it's done."

GALLIN WAITED for a cab at Broadway and 110th, outside an Italian restaurant on the corner, closed that night for a private party, its windows opaque with steam. Inside, Gallin could hear opera singers stirring the souls of winter revelers. *O solo mio*, a courageous tenor hurled into the air, confounding centuries of progress. Gallin exhaled, repeating the words.

TWELVE

Gallin's intent to borrow his grandson so that Bernardo could consecrate some perverse act of loyal, loving abandonment saw him Tuesday morning in a cold cab going uptown to visit Kiran. She was Bernardo's wife—or widow. His mind was rotten with Denmarkian doubt. Everything he did now had at least a whiff of turpitude, but only this foul part proposed to infect an innocent, Tyler, and it scratched at his soul. In a way what Bernardo wanted was beautiful. In a way so was the snake.

Though the building was designated 1160 Park Avenue, the green awning that stated this and shielded the entrance was not on Park but on 92nd Street—about a third of the way to Madison. A seemingly harmless bit of topographical dissonance, the address's duality irritated Gallin, signaling for him a larger, more serious problem wherein little, anymore, was called what it actually was. Indeed, everywhere he looked, he saw precision endangered. In business, for instance; in the scandal of the moment, Enron had obfuscated itself into a seven-billion dollar company, until it was revealed that there was no there there. Laxity with language had allowed it—nobody hearing what was not being said. Perhaps it began with job titles that had become obscurantist manifestos; Gallin recently operated on a man whose business card read "Contextual Visualization Assessment Specialist" and who, pressed, confessed to being an accountant. Jargon and its execrable vagaries, invented to exclude outsiders, now corrupted even the simplest exchanges. Regularly, even newspaper headlines—lifeblood of a republic—wanted parsing, translation. Even the elephant in the room, advertising, which would seem to need to be plain, promised fulfillment with such winsome abstractions that it said nothing at all. *Just do it, do more, you deserve a break today.* It was a communications collapse.

With places, the problem was especially bad. A couple of months earlier Gallin was driving in New Jersey when he realized that whole swaths of the state between Newark and Camden were apparently now a part of Princeton, stretching that desirable address for fifty miles along Route 1, well past credibility. It was a specious attempt to leech university prestige from the legacies of Scott Fitzgerald and Woodrow Wilson, Oppenheimer and Einstein. A sense of place was apparently a deep and fungible desire. There was Princeton Meadows and Princeton Courts and Princeton Oaks and Princeton Commons—none of them anywhere near the college town.

Irritated and disguising a limp, Gallin ducked in under the 92nd Street awning, out of the cold. The doorman greeted him familiarly, but with a formal respect bordering on grimness. Gallin had seen this man quite a bit since September. After the attacks he had quite gracefully assumed a sort of helpful chaplain's role in the fractured affairs of his shaken tenants, and Gallin had thought him a sturdy character. Trim and elegant with a thin mustache, he moved quickly but with a winning reserve. It suppressed, Gallin suspected, a congenital flair. His heels knocked the floor as if he battled an incipient tango. Gallin regretted not knowing his name, but it was too late to ask: they had their rapport.

"The penthouse, please, sir," Gallin said.

"Yes, Doctor. The lady is in. She is expecting you." His black eyes flickered. He reminded Gallin of an Argentine he had once watched a soccer game with in Buenos Aires. For ninety minutes the man had explained the majesty of the great Diego Maradona as if describing a saint. Life was better if you could see your gods.

"Let me ask you something," Gallin said. "Do people ever get confused about the address here? Does it cause problems—I mean, where the door is?"

"You mean on the street instead of the avenue? Oh, sometimes if there's a party the cabs will miss it. But not usually, Doctor," he answered cheerfully.

"Hmmph," Gallin chewed on this answer. "Has she been out today?"

"No, Doctor. But she was out yesterday for a little while with the little one. He was bundled like a mummy but they looked nice going out." He smiled with genuine sympathy, and gestured with his arm: "This way, sir."

Gallin walked alone down the parquet corridor to the elevator. A bouquet of orchids rose regally from a crystal vase on a lacquered console along one wall. The flowers were gorgeous, exuberant, although cut, and days from dying. Just for our pleasure, he thought, we kill them. The bouquet moved him to consider vaguely the passage of time, its rapidity, rapaciousness. In a quick vision he was a hand on a clock. Blood pounded in his head as he hung upside down, dressed in black, his head pointing at the six.

When the elevator door closed on him he had the sensation of being locked in a vacuum. The air-sucked silence felt like his coffin. He remembered this had been one of his dreams the night before. That boy's story of being buried alive had flicked some gruesome switch in him and he was forced now to add suffocation to his troubles. He had a hallucinatory fear that the elevator would burrow into the ground instead of rising. That it would bury him. But the car began its ascent.

Gallin took measure of himself in the elevator's smoked mirror wall. Dark reflections were flattering. He was still young, he considered. Young and vital. He was having troubles only because this was a troubled world, a troubled time. The sepia Gallin told more: he was a handsome man—as handsome, anyway, as he had ever been. He pulled his shoulders back, breathed deep. And he had just found a new lover. An exotic. One who shared his secrets, his own Sphinx. He was a lucky man, fortunate. But was Ana genuine? Or had he imagined her goodness? No, she had held his empty hand, kissed his chest. He hoped she could be trusted.

He gave his head a violent shake, as if to discharge water from his ears. His mind shook clear. He stared intently at himself.

In the next five seconds he had to change worlds again. He had to kill Bernardo in his mind, for when he got to Kiran they needed to know the same things, share the same world. And in her world Bernardo was dead. Gallin closed his eyes and put Bernardo in his own imaginary coffin. You're dead again boy, he said to himself. This time he took some pleasure in it.

The elevator doors cleaved and released him, opening directly into the penthouse. Gallin was met by the unexpected thrum of reggae music; it filled the space with beatific warmth. *Could you be—could you be—could you be loved?* Bob Marley's singers demanded to know, in voices that burned soft like sunsets. Again and again, the question. *Couldjubee, coojabee, cudjabee luvd? Coojahbee, cudjabee luvd?* It occurred to Gallin that the question could bear any amount of repetition. Then *Don't let them change-yah, ohhhh*—cried Marley himself, his voice an echo of some ancient deliverance.

KIRAN CAME swirling down the spiral staircase like the last water to the drain. She wore short denim shorts and a man's white ribbed sleeveless undershirt. She was barefoot, her dark hair loosely banded atop her head. Her skin was the pure pale of one who has forever disdained the sun. A familiar blast of excitement, then shame, knocked Gallin back. He had always fought a powerful physical attraction to this woman. Painfully, he suspected it was not a one-way emotion. During the grieving it had been particularly hard to have it there between them, whatever it was, because his most earnest efforts to console were always a half-sobbed breath or teardrop from impropriety. When he held her, her lashes would flutter against his cheek, tickling his skin, oppressing his heart. And in the first few months he held her often; she seemed to collapse utterly in his arms, lush and exhausted, tender and beaten, emptied of will. He had tried to think of her as his daughter, to remain bound by category, but she was not his daughter. Anyway, he had no experience with daughters. Her tears sometimes sailed down onto his lips. He took them on his tongue and savored them.

Years before at the Woodbrook house, he had walked in on her one summer morning lying naked on the bed, touching herself between her legs. He should have turned and run, but for four or five frozen seconds he could not. He stood motionless, mesmerized. She didn't jump, didn't cover up. She stayed silent. Her pale body, all one color even in summer, radiated against the mussed, periwinkle sheets. She simply stopped moving her hand and smiled at him.

What face he made in response he did not know, but he retreated quickly, murmuring *sorry, I—*. And sorry he was, good god, for the scene had tortured him since, if also it was a secret pleasure: the moment returned to him too often, almost whenever he smelled morning air slipping through a window screen. A thousand times his mind had considered this smile, yet it remained as enigmatic as the Mona Lisa's. Sometimes he decided it was an embarrassed smile, a natural enough reaction. Nervousness at being surprised: embarrassment. But there was something about it that wasn't abashed at all. Behind it was some other feeling, one of those other million emotions that don't yet have names. Gallin sometimes wondered if she'd told Bernardo. But how could she? She mustn't have. Again he wasn't sure, but his instincts told him the incident was between them only—between Gallin and Kiran—and somehow not unhappily.

Today as she came down the stairs her beautifully curved breasts in the clinging shirt were too visible, too present for his comfort. From breastfeeding they were fuller, even more demonstrative, and they thrust themselves into his consciousness as unstoppably as dreams. Their shape was as perfect, he saw, as ever, yet unsubtly magnified by new duty. Gallin thought about Kiran's breasts often, for he thought about them in surgery. Unfortunately, his son's wife's breasts were the ideal he aimed for whenever his patient's concern was beauty and shape rather than mere volume. It was a difficult situation. Gallin felt slimy, perverse about it at times. But he forgave himself his thoughts about her breasts. It was work: all art needs inspiration.

"Richard, P*apa*," she said landing hard on the second *pa*. She rarely called him that. "I'm so glad you're here. Thank god."

She had a wild look in her eyes, a blend of fright and remove, as if her mind had gone half-away to elude what alarmed it. Gallin thought the look was simply a result of her working. In his experience artists often looked a mess when they worked, distant and feverish. He remembered his friend Sudol when he first struck upon the idea for his glass art. He looked like a madman. But she grabbed him by the hand too brusquely, leading him in minor panic to the stairs she had just descended. She smelled of turpentine and perfume.

"You have to see this," she said. "It's been freaking me out."

The capacious apartment was done in a modern minimalist style, in chrome and black leather and etched glass, with pale wood floors. The bookshelves were constructed from perforated steel, reminding him of things he built with his erector set as a child, and the books were too neatly placed on them. Big art books from museums dominated the shelves. The walls were starkly white and adorned with Kiran's own paintings, layered constructions of thick paint that seemed very sad to Gallin—mournful, melancholic. People, however, bought them sometimes; she was represented by a well-known gallery, if not too vigorously. The work was similar in style to late Rothko—looking hard one could find landscapes in them, or seascapes or moonscapes—but in her paintings all colors appeared to be withering slowly toward rust. Gallin wasn't sure if she meant this effect, or even saw it. But the blues and the greens, even the basest black, gave an impression of retarded oxidation. Still the rust he perceived on the paintings, intended or not, was all that alleviated the oppressive industrial orderliness of this apartment, which to Gallin—who enjoyed overstuffed armchairs and comfortable clutter—was decidedly un-homey. It all looked to him like his kitchen, with its stainless subzero freezers, black iron burners, and the plain ivory-colored dishes.

137

Kiran herself gave him those monotonous new dishes after he'd finally chipped the last inviolate survivor among the floral-painted dishes he and Christa had received as a wedding gift in 1969. That plate was the last of anything from that year that had held on. It had become precious to him. When three years ago he'd chipped it, standing alone in his soulless kitchen, a tiny little chip, he surprised himself by smashing it immediately to the floor. Goodbye to all that, as if to say. It was on a winter morning like this one, cold and bright, except it was in the last century—when smashing something in America meant less.

He followed her up the stairs, watching her ass. The weight she'd added with the baby complemented her, though he now noticed that the tops of her arms were getting thicker. She had new strength there from lifting and carrying Tyler, but the muscles were wearing a soft fatty armor. She, too, would grow old.

The studio that Bernardo had built at the top of their sprawling apartment was one of the best rooms Gallin had seen in all of New York. It looked through two walls of giant windows out over the park to the great old buildings that lined Central Park West. At the rear of the room the two walls used for hanging space were painted a glossy black, giving the room a heft missing from the white-walled rooms below. Five paintings hung there, unchanged since his previous visit. They were in her usual style. New though, to his eyes, was a sculpture being worked on near the far windows. It was large, four or five feet tall. He couldn't get a good look, but from the back it appeared to be the start of a large head. It faced west and slightly south, gazing over the park and beyond. It gave the powerful impression of watching over the city, of omniscience.

Kiran pulled him over to the windows farthest from the sculpture.

"Look," she said, pointing out. Hovering in the crystalline sky was the MetLife blimp, so close it seemed you could hit it throwing a baseball. The blimp was remarkably still, almost immobile. It just hung in the air, massive. It was fantastic looking, its blue and white skin rippling occasionally from gusts of winter wind.

"Do you see it?" she asked him. Her voice, in agitation, matched her alarming eyes.

"What, the blimp?"

"Yes."

"I do, I see it. Snoopy One, I believe. Or Snoopy Two," he said cheerfully. Charles Schulz's self-possessed cartoon dog was the symbol of the Metropolitan Life Insurance Company, and consequently the symbolic copilot of these airships. Gallin had seen a lot of Snoopy during golf broadcasts. The broadcasters mentioned him every ten minutes it seemed during the golf.

"It keeps turning around, rotating, but not going anywhere. Wait until it turns again, it says on the other side *have you met life today*?"

"I've seen it."

"Well *why* is it here? Don't you think it's creepy—to be just hovering over the park like that all morning, not *doing* anything?"

"Maybe there's an event nearby. They're probably just getting some pictures."

"But Richard, don't you think it could be terrorists? I mean wouldn't that be the perfect thing to get a hold of the blimp with that morbid question written on it and spray poison all over New York with it? Isn't that just what they want to do? While we're all looking for a plane again? They could drop some anthrax spray into that wind and kill a million people."

She was near tears. Gallin found a zip-up sweatshirt on a hook by the stairwell and handed it to her. "Here, put this on. It's cold near the windows."

"But couldn't they? I mean how do we know who's driving that Snoopy? Why won't it move? Look, here it comes around again. I feel like they're asking us to read that question. 'You people who live in the sky while we live in caves, in the dirt.' Why do they do it? I don't think I'm better than they are. You know, like, have you met death today is what they really mean. Or will you? God, I'm going crazy."

She slipped on the sweatshirt. Gallin felt relieved at this.

"Thank god for this music," she said. "It calms us down. I had Tyler up here with me before and I swear to you he was scared of the blimp. That's how I first noticed it. He just started screaming, which he never does during the day. And, you know, nothing makes him happier than a balloon, so it's totally wrong for him to be scared of the blimp. It really makes you think something's wrong. And I called that stupid 311 line and they treated me like I was out of my mind. I said, well, if I'm out of my mind, why doesn't it move? Why doesn't it fly off?"

"Oh, sweetheart," he said, in his best fatherly tone. "It's okay." He rubbed her covered shoulder. "This is nothing to worry about, nothing at all. Where is Tyler anyway? I was hoping to see him. In fact, I was hoping to borrow him for a bit. Give you a break, take a little walk or something. It's not quite as cold out today as it's been."

"It feels freezing to me."

"Well, it's winter."

"Yes, well, he's asleep. I put him down. The music really works wonders on him. The louder it is, too, the quicker he goes. Isn't that strange? You want to see him? I can get you something to drink. Coffee?"

"Terrific. Yes, Kiran, thank you."

Downstairs again, Marley was saying to stand up for your rights. In the kitchen she poured the coffee from a nearly empty pot that had been sitting awhile, red light aglow. It was the dregs. The smell of burnt bean hit Gallin nastily in the nose. Steam rose up from the mug and yet she put it in the microwave. Uneasily, he sat down at the end of a long oval table. At the opposite end were piled two neat stacks of official looking paperwork.

"Milk?"

"Yes, you know."

"Sorry, yes I do."

She pulled open the microwave door almost as soon as she'd closed it and added milk to the mug. She put it down in front of him, too hot to drink. He noticed coffee rings on the table; they seemed of recent vintage. She must have drunk a whole pot already, he thought.

Kiran sat down next to him. Her hands, which she placed on the table, shook. She connected them. The gesture gave her a look of praying.

"Like I said, I thought I might take him on a walk," Gallin repeated, trying to get to his business.

Cupping his hands around the hot mug, Gallin warmed them. His leg ached from descending the stairs.

"Oh, but it is really cold today. I can feel it."

She closed her eyes and appeared to be trying literally to feel the cold outside. Gallin wondered what Kiran the artist would think if she could see herself. Would she think she was beautiful or sad? He looked at her eyelids. Where her long lashes grew, the lids plumped into a dark sensuous crescent. But otherwise these lids were painfully thin, so tender as to be almost translucent. Tiny veins wandered visibly through them, forming raw webs of pink. They must have been a meager aid in keeping out the world.

"It's really not as cold as yesterday," Gallin said. "If I told you what happened to me yesterday, and how cold I was, I don't think you'd believe it."

"What happened? Tell me."

"I would. I'd tell you if I thought it'd be interesting to anybody but me. But I'm afraid it wouldn't. Some things, I discover more and more, are like that. They seem so big, but only because it's happening to you."

"But some things *are* big," Kiran answered defensively. She jerked her foot under the table and kicked Gallin in his leg. The accidental boot sent a shiver of pain through him. "Oh, sorry," she said. "I'm sorry. I didn't think I kicked you that hard."

"No, you didn't. It was nothing. I had a charley horse earlier and you just gave me a little reminder. Nothing much."

"Oh."

He got up to add a bit more milk to his cup.

"Are you limping?" she asked him.

"Oh no, not at all. I told you a little charley horse. Age really."

141

"I'm terrified of it."

"Of what?"

"Age."

"Oh."

"Among other things," she said, trying to smile. "But yes, age is terrifying."

"I'd love to say you shouldn't be, but—"

"Shouldn't be terrified of it?"

"Yes, I would say you shouldn't—"

"But you're not a liar."

"Right. Not in this case, I suppose I'm not." Gallin, wanting to change the subject, asked, "How long has he been down?"

Kiran reached into a jewelry box on the table and took out a joint.

"Early," Gallin said, nodding at the joint.

"Time is pretty relative," she replied. "He's down now. Now's a good time."

She lit the joint and stood up, waving away the smoke with the same hand that held it. She took two quick hits and put it out. As she was putting it out she said, "You don't want any do you?"

She knew he would say no. He shook his head.

"Can you work, are you working?" he asked.

"A little. I'm doing something for Bernardo. It's upstairs."

"I think I saw that. It's different for you. I'm glad you can work. That's important."

"Is it?"

"I think it is," Gallin said.

"Not you?" she asked him, gesticulating as if with a scalpel, asking about his own ability to work. He felt familial toward her when she asked it.

"Oh, I'm ready now," he said. "It's just what I do—well it seemed particularly senseless for a while. I needed to back off."

"But didn't you tell me people wanted it more than ever, the surgery? After the 11th?"

"Yes, but I wasn't as sure about how much I wanted to give it to them. Like I said, there was a desire to back off."

"That's right, though, isn't it? To step back, I mean? It's appropriate."

"I think it is," he said.

Kiran lit the joint again and took another quick drag. The smoke smelled delicious to Gallin. "You want to go look at the baby?"

"Sure."

Tyler slept on his back, head turned to the side, a trickle of saliva glistening on his pudgy cheek and tiny chin. He wore a little knitted cotton cap, out from which peeked enchanting ringlets of black hair. Such a long journey for him ahead, Gallin thought. Till he's a man. Fifty years? Longer? How long does it take, Gallin wondered, to really become a man?

Gallin touched the boy's cheek. So soft! Of all the skin he touches, this he never feels.

"He was hard last night—up all through it. He always slept when Bernardo slept. They were on the same schedule, father and son. Early to bed, early to rise."

Gallin rubbed the small of Kiran's back. They gazed at the child.

"At night I hold him and rock him and look out the windows upstairs and—you know, we're on top of the world here, but it's so desolate. I just rock with the baby whimpering and I want to cry too but I can't." She turned away, and then back to face him with great intensity. She said: "I'm not sure I loved him, Richard. I'm not sure I loved Bernardo at all. I don't think there was anything real between us. I'm terrified there was nothing. I'm terrified of getting old and of being alone at the top of the world at night and knowing that I wasn't in love with my husband. What does that mean for Tyler, if I wasn't in love with his father?"

"Oh, Kiran. It's okay, it's okay," Gallin told her. "It's the shock that makes these thoughts so sharp. That's all."

Kiran pushed her face into his chest, wrapped her arms around his waist. She felt as supple as the baby.

"Even when there's no real cause for doubt," he continued, whispering, stroking her neck where her hair was pulled up.

"There are circumstances so drastic sometimes that your mind will do anything. Try not to think about it."

The image of a widowed Kiran filled Gallin's mind with sorrow. He asked himself, surprised by the question: Should he marry her? It was a notion he believed he borrowed from antiquity, from the Old Testament, or Ovid or Homer. Somewhere the father assumed responsibilities vacated by the son. But was it honorable, this duty? Or was it simply perverse? In America in 2002 the answer was definitely perverse. But Gallin also knew that the real answer floated on the continuum of time, that it was the concern of cultures.

She pulled herself away from him, wiping her eyes. Her sad, luminous face grew rigid.

"Do you want to see what I'm working on?" she asked. "The sculpture?"

"I think I saw it."

"No, you have to touch it. He was your son. You'll see. It means something."

She started pulling him toward the stairs. On the way up she started to talk again, but in a strange faraway voice, as if her emotions had dried up suddenly in a wind.

"I understand what you're saying," she said coolly. "But I think it's different what's happening to me. I don't think these feelings I have are common at all. See, so much of it was about money."

"Are you okay for money?" Gallin quickly interjected. "Do you need help with anything?" He had a strong feeling that talking about money now could come to no good, and he wanted to head off the conversation if he could. Money insinuated itself everywhere, but in some places it made a nastier mess than others. "I was under the impression that everything was settled very well," he said. "With Bentley, and the agencies. Not to mention amounts. But I thought your comfort was assured. I thought it was in the millions."

"My comfort assured," she repeated bitterly.

"I'm sorry, that was terrible. I only meant financially."

"I haven't decided to settle everything just yet," she said. They were upstairs again now. The sun spilt abundantly through the windows. The blimp was gone. "You saw all those papers on the kitchen table. Some lawyers are saying I could get a lot more and—oh, it makes me sick. But what really makes me sick is that I think I *should* try to get more. I feel that's the right thing. Because with Bernardo, you know, it *was* all about the money. Not just with him, but with us. It's embarrassing. It's vulgar, but part of my attraction to him *was* the money. He knew that. So now that he's gone, why shouldn't I replace him as exactly as I can? And that's with money. You can't look at me like I'm a whore because he knew it and he liked it. He wanted me to like him for the money. He wanted to fucking *be* money. And he achieved it because after a while I could hardly distinguish him from the money. You know what his favorite thing to do was? To pay me. To give me cash and say do this and do that now. It was his biggest turn-on. Now this is the first time I've seen him separate from the money, now that he's dead, but the money lives on. It was bigger than he was. It lasted through the attacks. When I think of him now, he seems so weak. I don't even know if he had character."

Now she was crying, but Gallin did not reach out to her. She walked over to the sculpture. On the side Gallin hadn't seen at first, half of Bernardo's face was rendered large and beautifully.

"Do you think he could have been a martyr, Richard?" she asked, wiping tears on her sleeve. "I mean, did he die for something?"

"I don't know."

"If I could think he was a martyr, if I could have a reason I could live with, you know?"

Gallin put his hand on the head of the statue, this five-foot plaster head of his only son. It was surprisingly warm.

Feeling, sliding his knowing fingers along its enlarged features, Gallin realized it was good. It was genuine, a rarity. It had real warmth, literal warmth, so different from her rusting canvasses. If this was a portrait of weakness, then beauty was not in strength.

"I don't think you should take Tyler today, Richard. He had a tough night. Maybe another day, okay?"

"Yes, I think you're right," he said. "Today is not the day for it. I've got to be going anyway. I've been here longer than I should have already."

THIRTEEN

That Tuesday afternoon Gallin's former nurse, Peter Gunsenhauser, was scheduled to meet his old boss at the White Horse Tavern, the West Village spot where Dylan Thomas famously drank his last dozen whiskeys. Indeed, pictures of the fallen dipsomaniac poet decorated every wall, having helped to kill him apparently a point of lasting institutional pride.

Peter arrived early and selected a lambent table by the window. The tavern was in a viscous lull, muddling through those groaning hours between the end of lunch and the arrival of evening, hours when other cultures were smart enough to take a siesta. At the bar were only five: a young dark-haired couple in blue jeans, speaking quiet French and staring deeply into each other's eyes, his hand on her knee, their pink drinks untouched; and three senior wizened alcoholics, presumably on their regular stools, having the look of been-there merchant marines, sea salts down to their gray scruff, paying their own sort of homage to the dead poet with their bourbon shots and short beers.

Slouched off by the waitress station, a bed-headed young bartender read the *Post* and rubbed a tomato juice stain on his shirt with a club-soda-soaked rag. Peter turned his back on this crew, thinking of that Hopper painting. Outside the air was crisp and clean; pedestrians' breath fogged and vanished; the sun beamed with wintry radiance.

Not twelve blocks to the south workers at Ground Zero were still digging out round the clock from the rubble. Eight-hour shifts gave way to another set and then a third, and then a new day began: the clearing did not stop. The men and women who dug and deciphered in the fresh mass grave believed in their souls that they did noble work, and were driven by this sense to near exhaustion in the endeavor. All New York, all the world, watched them. What would they find? How quickly could the giant recover? And with these answers unknown, emotion lay raw and burning on the very surface of the ground—stoked not infrequently by a discovered shin bone or an eyeball or a simple tuft of hair—so that this work was a hot relentless reminder of the great violation that had occurred.

Yet, there were already signs of the first fissure in the new togetherness of the city, a togetherness, tellingly, portentously, built in a day. Even as the dust clouds rose over the crater, and the sweat and the tears dripped onto the ground to sanctify the slaughtered, there were those who wanted to move on, who saw it was time. For though there remained some dreamers who dreamed that survivors were still trapped and miraculously alive in pockets beneath the wreckage, and others like them who needed to find some piece of their departed for closure, it was understood by most that the pit would soon transform into a construction site, however hallowed. That the looking and searching had reached the end of its efficacy. That any body found now would be as dead as Lincoln. This latter group, rationalists anxious to move things forward, counted among its core the new billionaire mayor, and he quickly and characteristically set about separating the emotions from the job at hand.

The mayor's pragmatism scalded, predictably, the open pain of the firefighters, who led the rescue effort—as it was still being illogically called—and they made fierce emotional claims about needing to continue the search for their lost and heroic brethren, the sacrificial storm troopers who'd run up the burning stairs on the day of disaster. The passion of these men tugged at the mottled pink heart of the city, which was as exposed and broken as the men themselves. The controversy made the mayor a villain, until someone from his office leaked the notion to the press that the gallantry of the men might have as much to do with the staggering overtime pay they were collecting as with their claims of high and noble purpose. One fights fire with fire, so to speak, and in New York that fire was always money. It was a shame, the greed, but it was comforting as well for being recognizably selfish and human: the unity of New York, of America, could not last forever.

Gazing out onto Hudson Street, Peter duly noted that it was another marvelous day to be alive. This was a habit of daily affirmation he'd got himself into after so much AIDS counseling had produced little else of use, but lately he found himself forgetting more often. He could go days now, he noticed, without remembering to be overtly grateful for drawing breath. Instead, what he'd been thinking was that he didn't feel sick, didn't feel sick at all. In fact, he had never felt stronger. It had been more than a year since he was diagnosed, and he felt more fit now than at any other time he could remember.

Fifteen, twenty years ago, a full year of life with HIV was on the outside of prognosis: hope then could hold only a hundred days, maybe two-hundred. Peter had watched friends wither and die as fast as autumn leaves. He had been lucky during those years, avoiding contagion. But talk about terror. There was no such thing as terror until you've looked into the vacant eyes of a plague. To his mind, much of what September 11th had done was to make all New Yorkers feel the way gay men felt back around 1984: that they were being killed simply for the way they lived. Attacked for being who they were. No, terror was nothing new to gay men, he thought.

The sun shifted and the window gave Peter back his own reflection. He admired it. He was not handsome, but he felt he presented himself with integrity. He admired his upper lip, where he had shaved off his mustache when he realized that he wore it as a badge of something—a vague statement of membership in his dubious community—and that it ultimately obscured him. Now his face was fresh, forthright. He thought it matched his insides. He looked good—or not so much good, but right, correct. This was him, disease and all.

149

Of course, the difference between having the virus now and having it twenty years ago was the pills, the little soldierly triumvirate he swallowed daily like a priest took the host: AZT, 3TC and efavirenz. Pure science, a thing of beauty. The cocktail, as some demented antagonist had labeled it, cruelly getting both the words cock and tail in there, and at the same time making it sound like a cause for celebration, a little cosmopolitan meet. *Let's have a cocktail.* Well that part was right: it was a cause for celebration.

Now another affirmation occurred to him, and he spoke it silently to himself: Thank god for health insurance. Thank god for Nicky and his job at *New York*, however much it tortured his lover's already tortured soul to work there, to write the drivel. What bad timing it had been for them too. Losing his job had forced Nick into staying at his—the opposite of what they'd planned. Just before the diagnosis, Nick had been going to quit the magazine to work on his writing and Peter was going to support them both. Now this meeting with Gallin—a surprise—revived his hope. Perhaps they could do it after all.

Peter had a good feeling, thinking the doctor had finally realized how small a risk his condition actually presented. He hoped Gallin was coming down to ask him back to work. Perhaps the loss of Bernardo had made him rethink things. He'd heard from Janine that he was having a hard time of it: business was off and he didn't seem to be himself. People certainly seemed to be thinking differently, changing priorities. One of the salts got up and played a Johnny Mathis Christmas song on the jukebox. Peter understood; he hated to let the holidays go as well.

Gallin was no longer disguising his limp when he peglegged like a tall pirate into the White Horse, looking around anxiously. A half-hour late, he had cause to worry that Peter wouldn't wait for him—the latter didn't owe him any favors. But Peter quickly held up his hand, smiling. Gallin smiled in response, relieved. He was acutely aware of the muscles in his face building the smile. It was the first in a while.

"Peter, no, please, sit down, I'm so sorry," Gallin explained. "For being late, I mean."

"Oh, Dr. G," Peter said. "Time is moving slowly around here anyway."

He indicated the empty seats all around him. To his surprise, a waitress sprang immediately to the table, out of nowhere.

"Give us a minute, please," Gallin said, waving her off, smiling again, his smile like a new toy. "Peter, you look good. Terrific. How do you feel?"

"Oh, never better, to be honest. Have never felt anything but great the whole time."

"That's fantastic. Tremendous."

Gallin slid out of his long cashmere coat while seated, letting it lay casually on the back of his chair, as if he might only stay a minute. Again the waitress appeared with alacrity, asking if she could take his coat. As she spoke to the doctor her bright eyes grew larger, and she moved her head in a way that made her dark hair bounce almost imperceptibly. Peter was pleased with this new level of service, pleased that he had chosen a place where they would be so well treated. It did not bother him—indeed he did not quite notice—that until Gallin sat down his own jacket had hung cumbersomely on the back of his own chair. No one had asked to take it for him. Now the waitress took both coats away.

"Something's different," Gallin said, regarding Peter carefully, searching his face. "Have you lost weight?"

Gallin meant this as a compliment but it was a tender spot for Peter. He had, but he was worried that the weight loss might be perceived as a pejorative result of the HIV. Rather it had come from working out, performing some of the exercises Nick had given him—boxing routines.

"I have, yes," he said, his deep nasal voice pulling Gallin toward him. "Believe it or not, I've been learning how to box," he said more quietly, a bit embarrassed by this, as if it would sound too unbelievable. He then made a soft fist and, as a joke, threw a little feint of a jab. It was a gesture born of social awkwardness. He

151

was conscious that it was a flaccid little movement, more faggot than fighter. He laughed at himself as though to say oh, well, that's where it is so far, my boxing. But Gallin recognized the big sure hands he had seen so many times, hands that for years had handed him just what he needed. He saw in them an emblem of simpler, easier times. It was odd to see them in a fist.

"No, still it's something else. Yes, you had a mustache. A big one."

Gallin signaled for the waitress with a flick of his hand. He ordered a martini, up and dry.

"Thank you, dear," he said to the waitress, after she'd promise to bring it "right away, sir."

"Dr. G, I hope you got my note and the flowers."

"That was very kind of you, Peter. I'm sorry I haven't written my thanks. It is on a list of things to do that seems to get longer as I tackle it. The flowers were lovely. I was touched by your words. Thank you for taking the time."

"Oh, of course."

"Peter, listen, I'm sorry about the way things worked out," Gallin started. "I'm not sorry about what I had to do—I still don't see where I had a choice." Gallin wished he could control this in himself, the constant defense of his position. He remembered vaguely once not feeling that he had to defend everything.

Peter's spirits sank; so it was not to hire him back that he'd come.

"But I appreciate the way you understood and handled it. And I'm enormously pleased to see you're doing well. You look healthy." The waitress delivered his drink, and a hot tea for Peter. "What is this Christmas music?" Gallin asked her. "Has time actually stopped in here?" he asked cheerfully.

She laughed and nodded over her shoulder to the salts, who were swaying to Mathis's Christmas past.

Gallin stabbed an escaped olive with a little plastic sword and ate it. The gin was ice cold, quickening. Along with the smell of Peter's tea it made him think of India. He raised his glass.

"Peter, I have a proposition for you." They clinked. Gallin took a fortifying swallow. "It is going to sound strange, mysterious even. And it is."

Peter had meant to ask him about the limp, but he'd forgotten. This was a strange meeting. He had never seen Gallin outside of his milieu, and now limping and swallowing straight gin in the middle of the afternoon he cut a strange, unfamiliar figure. Overly cordial, reckless, his eyes charged with dubious mirth, Gallin seemed utterly changed. What had happened? Was it only Bernardo?

"If I tell you this," the doctor continued, "I will have opened a box I cannot close again, do you understand? And it is only on instinct that I feel I can do this with you. Above all it seems to me you are trustworthy, a—"

God, what is this confession going to be? Peter wondered. He was uncomfortable. But he was also charmed. He was flattered. Were they peers suddenly, he and his old boss? Should he call him Richard? Did Gallin come to speak with a friend? That was better than getting the old job, this business of being elevated.

Gallin continued, "Are you? Am I right in thinking that I can open this box in front of you? Tell me that I am. I need to be able to speak to you in confidence."

Gallin felt that he was talking too fast, that he might try to sound a little cooler. But he did not have a better plan than this. He had to appeal to Peter's honor. And honor was always—in his experience—touched best by hyperbole. Deep down Gallin believed that Peter would rather be in on a secret than expose one. Gallin took a swallow and signaled the waitress.

"Yes, I mean, of course," Peter replied. "Anything that you would tell me would be—"

"Yes?" the waitress interjected.

"I'll have a turkey sandwich, like the club, but without the bacon and the lettuce. Toasted, please. Peter what do you want?" Gallin asked brusquely.

153

Now Peter wondered if Gallin was okay. The man was in the middle of trying to exact a grave promise of fealty, and he calls over the waitress. His attention span seemed paper thin.

Gallin's interest was to move things along. Though he was asking for something serious, he did not want his request dwelt upon like a serious thing. He found it was often better to back people into serious commitments. He'd come on too strong at first, he thought.

"I'll have the chicken sandwich and no tomatoes unless you have good tomatoes, because the tomatoes are always terrible this time of year," Peter told the waitress. He hoped she would discourage skipping them, reporting instead that they had wonderful tomatoes, even in the winter, red and juicy.

Instead she repeated, writing on her pad, "No tomatoes." She looked at Gallin, made her eyes wide again, "Can I bring you another martini, sir?"

He demurred with a wave, winningly, without a word. She scampered. He was all charm and brimstone.

"Okay, here it is, Peter. On occasion I do, as you know, some surgery that is very confidential. Well, it's secret, is what it is. This job fits into that category, and I need you for it. It's tomorrow night. And whatever you discover when you get there, you'll need to take with you to your grave—may that be a far, far, far off place, the grave," he said, raising his glass. "To your health."

"But Dr. G, why—I mean how is it that—I can assist you if you still believe that I—"

"This is a special case," Gallin interrupted. "I realize the odds of your infecting—I mean of any patient being infected with the virus in the O.R. are miniscule. I understand that, I've always understood it. It's nine million to one or something, like the lottery. But to knowingly keep you on, and run that risk, however small, is not something that I can do, not something I could do. This, though, is once, just once."

"Is it a celebrity or something? Is that why it needs to be done at night?"

"No, and it's not a mobster either, or anything like that. You can curb your imagination. There's nothing sexy about this one. It's just a job, but a pretty thorough transformation we're after. Everything, really, that can be done to a face. Hard stuff, a long theatre. Can I count on you?"

"Well, yes, I think so, I—"

"Here's the deal. *Again*. You can't tell anybody. I mean anybody. Not your lover, nobody. And it can't be a problem that you're going to be out all night. Is that going to be a problem? Because there can't even be any suspicion around this, understand?"

"It sounds very dark, Dr. G. Is everything all right? I mean, it sounds like you've got some bad stuff going on."

"Listen Peter, I need to know. I can tell you one more thing, but it's not the most important thing. The job is worth ten thousand to you. One night's work, and a lifetime of forgetting it. How's that? Can you do it?"

"Absolutely." Peter's nasal tone could have great authority.

"And this Adams won't know?"

"No, but how did you even know his name, my Nicky?"

Gallin's brain froze; he grabbed another olive with his fingers.

"Oh, I don't know, you must have mentioned him to me," Gallin said, buying time. "Yes, right, wasn't his name on the flowers you sent?"

"No."

God, no, he thought.

"Oh, maybe it was Janine then. You know she talks about you a lot. She and Annie miss you."

The sandwiches came. The tomatoes on Gallin's were red as China.

"Peter, I hate to do this, but I have to run." He took two enormous bites of his sandwich and started wrapping two of the triangles in his napkin. "We'll start the prep at nine. Please be there by eight-thirty. You can expect we'll go seven hours or so."

He took out a hundred-dollar bill and threw it on the table. "Your money will be in cash too, so bring something to carry it in."

Gallin was still chewing, when the waitress met him with his coat near the door. He stuffed his badly wrapped lunch into his deep side coat pocket, and felt in the other for his gloves.

He had to wait as a group of about a dozen deaf kids came in, their tour guide signing slowly with frigid hands, no doubt telling these wordless of how this would be an excellent place to die, if you were a poet.

FOURTEEN

In the master bedroom of Gallin's house in Woodbrook, Andrea stood naked with her back to the full-length mirror. She exhaled utterly, expelling, she hoped, the poisons of age. Then she craned her neck to look at herself from behind. The view dejected her. Though she was healthy and well-proportioned, she could not see it. She saw only the number forty, an age, coming at her like a bullet train.

Without inhaling again, she cast out another tiny toxic breath. There, out, she thought. Adieu. She'd been in the house alone only two days since Gallin had left on Sunday morning. She'd had high hopes for the time, picturing a peaceful refuge. But solitude for her was loneliness.

Looking back, she gripped the bottom right cheek of her ass and found too much flesh there. She pinched it, inches of it, glumly. Still it was not so much the inches as the way they were sinking. Flat at the top, her previously enviable ass now flared down into two regrettable bulges, like those plastic bags goldfish came in. Thank god I'm riding, she thought. But if it was over with Richard, there went that too. The rented horse, Mr. Hildy, the fine high boots that did so much to elongate her, the saddle perch, the rustic morning gallops with the giant engine of animal straddled beneath her—all gone, another packet of satisfaction and sensation banished to the past. Bonnie country life would recede as all her victories had receded. She couldn't afford on her own to even rent up here now, not anymore—you'd think it was the Hamptons with what they were asking. She'd missed her chance again, she was sure. Perhaps it was a thousand chances by now. She was too damn tired to take another.

She let go of her ass and sighed. Closing her eyes, she wriggled her neck to crack it, gratified by the chain of small spinal explosions. She bent down to touch her toes. She was amazingly limber, and she wrapped her palms all the way around her heels, pushing her head down between her thighs, which were slightly bowed. Pressure gathered in her sinuses as she peeked up into herself, pleased by how tidy things were there, how neat. Between her legs she seemed young yet. Against her cool thigh she pressed her nose, smelling the perfume daubed there, and with burning hamstrings and thighs redolent of roses, she had again the momentary but beautiful dream that time would stop. That it had done so.

Her only company, the dogs, lay sleeping on the bed, exhausted from a morning chasing squirrels. Their chests heaved drowsily with their breathing. Looking at them she recalled how Richard liked to say "Let sleeping dogs lie." He said it, she realized, almost every time he saw them dozing and the phrase now began to irritate her in the extreme. She wondered what it meant. She knew what it was supposed to mean. But what did it mean, really? To let sleeping dogs lie? It made her unaccountably angry now that he said it—and so often.

Wanting to undo the phrase, she clapped loudly. When this failed to rouse, she called their names. "Barney! Baby!" she called, at first gently. Still she got no response. When she stepped up onto the bed with them, the firm mattress bent a little beneath her concentrated weight. Slowly she started to bounce on it, to jump up and down. It was something she had never done. As a child, it had been forbidden. Naked still, she held her breasts tight against her chest. "Wake up, puppies!" she yelled out. Her voice was high-pitched, strident. It was a poor vessel for joy, though joy was in it. "Wake up, doggies! Wake up, sleeping dogs! Barney! Baby! Wake up! Sleeping dogs shouldn't lie!"

Barney became ecstatic. He joined the trampolining, thrusting his long face gleefully between her legs, timing his leaps to push his nose into her descending groin. Andrea laughed at him, simple creature. The harder she came crashing down, the greater was her

158

resultant catapult skyward. She tried to go higher and higher. Blood hurtled through her, oxygen danced evangelically in her lungs: beneath her flying feet the grim world lost all claim on her.

Baby, unmoved, alighted from this reckless paradise to seek a golden square of sunlight on the floor. There she tumbled on her side, closing her big brown indifferent eyes. The shaft of light that shone on her filled with frenzied dust.

Sixty miles to the south, the basement of Gallin's townhouse excluded the sun even on brilliant winter mornings, and in its stead dull track lighting shone on Bernardo, who, waiting for his new life to begin, was lying on a sofa looking through Plato's *Republic*. He'd found it in a low bookshelf that housed a bunch of his old high-school books, paperbacks that despite being mainly unread nevertheless looked worn, their cheap yellowing pages underlined where a teacher must have read a passage aloud, offering clues about the content of some long-forgotten test.

Looking at the books now, he saw the education he had forsaken would have made him a well-read man. Or if not that, at least a man intimate with desolation. On the shelf sat *Jude the Obscure*, Anne Frank, *Dubliners*, *Long Day's Journey into Night*, Swift, *Lear*, and *The Tempest*. There was Orwell and D. H. Lawrence, Emily Dickinson and Joseph Conrad. So many young people had read these same damn books, he thought, for how many years, and yet everyone kept on making the same mistakes. What good could they be?

Tossing Plato aside, Bernardo reached for *Brave New World*. It seemed a pertinent title for him—better than *The Loneliness of the Long Distance Runner*, which was next to it. He was not running. Of this he assured himself again.

On the inside cover was scrolled in his distant high school hand: "Huxley took acid! READ." But the first paragraph failed to grab him and somehow this book didn't have the advantage of underlined passages either. It landed on the Plato.

When by noon his father hadn't returned, Bernardo determined that the old man was not coming with Tyler. It had been too much to ask, he realized, to see the boy. It was wrong, and he felt about half human as he hid out in this damp cellar, for having requested it in the first place. Bernardo was angry with himself. He was angry that after all this time he did not know quite who he was. Angry that years before he had entered a cowardly bargain and chosen to be *neat*, that he had locked himself up that way. And he was disgusted with himself, too, because he was no longer in love with his wife. His marriage had meant a great deal to him—it, at least, had been born of honest emotion—and to feel that love drain off, to watch it become as meaningless, as false as the rest of life made him sick. That day on which he supposedly died, he had felt dead enough already, numb.

He took stock of himself again. There was much he despised. He was incessantly proving himself. Though it was a result of his insecurities, it became manifest as superiority. He was always trying for wit and edge. Conversations became contests. He was always vigilant for an advantage he might create. He loathed this in himself. He wanted to be pure.

In the new life, he hoped desperately that he would not be this way anymore, but rather relaxed, self-possessed, contented with things as they were. Why did he act as he did? No show of superiority made him feel better, or smarter, so why? It was something he seemed not to be able to control. He wanted honestly, desperately to escape it. And he believed he was capable, because he believed it was nurture and not nature that accounted for the petty awfulness in him. He was convinced that when he left behind the circumstances—the city, the money slogging, the envy that fueled a market economy and crept like worms into one's brain—he would walk peacefully in the woods, at one with the other creatures, knowing the names of all the trees.

He decided to shave. To prepare his face for its transformation. In the bathroom the steam rising from the sink softened him, stealing some of his bodily tension. He dragged the triple-bladed razor across his cheek, over his throat.

160

It took him a good half hour to shave it all. His face, when it stared back at him so denuded, surprised him. He looked like a different person, as if he'd already begun his metamorphosis. It was going to be a journey—to slough off this mundane disguise and become himself. But it would be a triumph! Toweling off in the steam, the water left to run, a strange activity suggested itself to him. He dropped to his knees in front of the sink. "Dear God," he uttered importunately, beginning something, but that was all he said. And he stood up.

A HALF mile away God was also being queried from a twelve-room duplex on Fifth Avenue, where eighty-eight-year-old Lester Rhodes was conversing easily with the same benevolent deity to whom he'd spoken freely all his life. Rhodes was no stranger to prayer—though his praying was more intrinsic than extramural. He hardly knew, most of the time, when he prayed. One consulted God quite naturally during the course of living.

Rhodes's wife, Cicely, was preparing to give him a few minutes peace—after hours of nervous conjugal observance. About her leaving, Rhodes was of two minds: he desired her company just now more than ever, but he craved solitude as much. She had tended to him officiously since he took to his bed at noon; and finally, after a campaign of reproach over his weak appetite, she was going down to the kitchen to ask Millie to bring the soup he'd agreed reluctantly to eat. When she left it would be his first moment alone since early that morning, when he'd recognized a fact that troubled him much less than he expected: he was dying.

"Darling," he said. "Darling, I still feel a bit lazy this afternoon. But I'd like to read, I believe, with the sunlight. Before you go would you draw back the curtains for me please, dear?" She had closed them earlier while he tried to nap.

Since it was not her husband's custom to take an early nap—though he sometimes sneaked late catnaps in his study—she was surprised by the sight of him putting on his pajamas at noon, readying for bed. She tried for nonchalance, but it worried her.

161

When she had closed the curtains, as the sunlight collapsed on her, her husband had thought what a beautiful woman she was. They had been married sixty-one generally happy years. They had taken their vows seriously. And though he normally resented being coddled he was happy today to let her do for him, fussing as she did, closing the curtains to assure his comfort, henpecking him about soup. He knew that purpose was her weapon against life's vagaries.

But with the curtains closed he found in the daytime darkness that he did not want to sleep. Instead he lay still with his eyes closed, flipping through the thick book of his memory. To his delight, pages appeared that had for years been missing—or had been simply too dark to see, the obliterating rot of age spilt over them like squid's ink. Now everything was illuminated. He turned through pages of his wedding, the war, his son's birth, the hospitals, the Woodbrook house—all things close to home, he realized—before his mind settled finally on the first tree he had ever climbed, a giant sycamore in his Massachusetts backyard. To have climbed it was perhaps the best of all he had done, though he had been one of the first Americans to arrive at Dachau, and he had married the woman of his dreams and they had made a son together, however grossly troubled. But the golden sycamore, its jointed limbs meandering sideways over the neighbors' fences, stood imperious. Of all things, surprisingly, it won the cover of the book of his life.

The fall Rhodes took on Friday, running into Gallin, had knocked the balance out of him and it was not coming back. On the weekend he'd struggled to walk. He hid this by pretending to be engaged beyond distraction with a novel of Balzac's. In fact he'd only stared at the book while an oceanic static played in his ears. Twice he vomited, another condition he'd managed to conceal from Cicely. But by Tuesday he could no longer fake it. He had to lie down in his bed. For all the time he had spent in hospitals, he did not want to go to a hospital. Always an expert diagnostician, he was certain he was bleeding in his brain, in which case little could be done.

Now with Cicely having again thrown open the curtains, the sun shone brightly through the window. Light splashed against the familiar objects in the room, which presented themselves to his beaten eyes with unusual clarity. The antique clock on the wall seemed almost alive, its ticking a metronome for his heart.

—God, Rhodes said, we have made a good run of it, wouldn't you say?

God said: indeed we have, Lester.

—And you'll take care of Cicely, I know. I can't think of her alone here.

Of course, God said. There are plans, as you know.

—Oh, I know but sometimes I wonder. I apologize, but I do.

God laughed. You are forgiven that, He said.

—What about our boy, though? Our son? Why was it that way? Why so sick?

Still you loved him.

—Yes, of course. And Cicely loved him. But You never brought him—we never brought him peace.

You gave him what you had, Lester.

—Yes, but never happiness. Always constant pain.

He is not unhappy now, God said. He never meant to hurt you, Lester. He only wanted to be as I am, but I gave him not the patience for that.

—But why? Forgive me now, but I know what today brings, God, and so I am bold. Why did you not give my son the patience?

But you understand the answers to these questions, Lester.

—Yes, I suppose. I have fashioned my reasons, anyway, in order to live.

I have watched you.

—I feel that. But the suffering.

That too, you understand.

—I'm not very sure of that.

What do you understand?

—That there is no difference between the suffering and the happiness.

I see, said God. Though God did not say this was true.

163

—So this was all, Rhodes said. I suppose it was a lot.

More than most, Lester. You had many gifts.

—And the soup? Will I get to eat the—

But he died then in mid-question, interrupting his pleasant talk with his God. As he died the bright window filled with shadowy gloaming, the westerly sun eclipsed by the MetLife blimp as it sailed above Fifth Avenue.

Had Kiran Gallin been looking out from her rooftop studio, she might also have seen the blimp that had so alarmed her casting its Benedictine shadow over the last light of Lester's life, but she'd turned inward. Instead she stared at her half-finished creation, the giant head of her dead husband. Something which she could not account for, something mysterious, had dictated its extravagant size, which seemed alternately preposterous and powerful to her. She stroked it lovingly. Only today had she become cognizant that the head was taller than her whole body. Until Richard had come, she hadn't noticed. But his being so tall and walking around in the studio changed her perspective. Only differences in height brought one's own into perspective, and Kiran realized that the more time she spent alone lately, the larger she felt. Compared to Tyler, of course, she was a giant.

The work on the finished half of the sculpture was as good an execution of her art as she had yet accomplished. This head, she knew in some very clear place, was as good a piece as she had ever made. It moved beyond, in that indescribable way, where she had been able to go with the paintings. And as this graceful understanding arose in her, it whispered something more, too: the head was finished. The work was complete. It would remain half-sculpted. The dawning of this knowledge was why she didn't see the ominous blimp, or notice the equally haunting broad-winged hawk that swept with anomalous urban majesty past her windows, a bloodied pigeon hanging from its talons.

She saw neither because she was in the trance that artists sometimes enter when a work has divulged the secret that it is finished. It was a trance comprised of postpartum sadness, of pride and wonder, of deep embarrassment, of fear of failure, of contribution, of continuum, and of analysis. The last was where the artist asked herself: what does the finished piece mean? An answer rarely arrived whole, but questions suggested one. Indeed, as she faced the sculpture, Kiran heard an odd, chant-like jingle of queries. It rang in her head like a nursery rhyme:

Is it wrong? Is it new? Wondered the jingle.

Will it end? Is it through?

Which nonsense was quickly followed by:

Was it whole? Was it true?

Was it me?

And then the last, which she stole, giving the work its title:

Was It You?

DOWNTOWN AT the White Horse, Peter Gunsenhauser, using the change from Gallin's hundred, was leaving the kind of prodigious tip he never left but always wanted to. A nurse, he felt a certain kinship with waitresses.

In the fifteen minutes since Gallin dashed, Peter had imagined a hundred ways to spend the ten thousand dollars he would earn the following night. Most of these were dreamy plans to purchase succor for his lover, Nick. A week in South Beach sparkled in his imagination like pink sand at first light. St. Barts, Aruba, and Negril meandered sweetly through his mind, a medley of paradisiacal tropical beauty poached from pictures in magazines. While he fantasized, Peter also worked an equation. It read blank = serenity, and he plugged into the blank space each destination as he conjured it, vowing to whisk his Nicky away immediately to whichever Eden fit the equation best.

Not since leaving Ohio as a young man had Peter felt the need to get away so pressing. It would do them both much good. Lately, Adams often woke in the middle of the night, cursing at some dreamt culprit in a voice edged with violence. And the episodes had grown worse just in the past week, preceded by spasms that were like exorcistic eruptions. Nicky had had a hard life, Peter knew, but something was really after him now, eating at his insides. Something more than the post–9/11 pall, he thought. He considered that it was just plain frustration: Adams had been writing feverishly, even more than usual, and still only *New York* had seen fit to publish him. Thin rejection notices arrived almost daily in their mailbox. And since protocol required a self-addressed stamped envelope with every submission, the returns, addressed in his own hand, the stamps licked by his own tongue, made it seem that he constantly rejected himself.

His literary efforts rebuffed, a monotonous destiny as a hack for hire, trumpeting cardboard musical ponies that couldn't run, must have gnawed at him. And there was something else going on, too: Peter suspected that Adams had a kind of secret project going. Probably, Peter thought, Adams slaved over yet another attempt at the Great American Novel, hoping by keeping it quiet to work without expectations. Or maybe it was a memoir. This thought was a revelation. Work on a memoir of the life of Nick Adams would account for the demons he was confronting at night, and for the increased jitteriness Peter had noticed during the day. That must be it, Peter thought, Nicky was writing a memoir. That could be wonderful, if harrowing. It was just the kind of thing that sold. He was, of course, oblivious to the fact that Adams's clandestine work was instead an exposé of Richard Gallin, meant to avenge Peter himself. How brave it was, Peter thought, of Nicky to confront his past.

BUT ADAMS, that afternoon, needed none of the sympathetic consideration he was being given as he galloped through Bergdorf Goodman in pursuit of a perfect silk tie, and perhaps a new shirt. Dr. Richard Gallin, Bernardo, even Peter were miles from his mind—and his crooked face wore a pure joy that made him seem almost classically handsome. In his breast pocket he carried a thin envelope that had arrived earlier that afternoon. It vouchsafed incomparable news: a first-rate literary agent had agreed to

166

take him on as a client. Indeed, the agent had written ecstatically about the ninety pages Adams sent her representing half the tale of his childhood on the "seesaw/chainsaw" of foster care. If Adams could promise a second half on par with the first, she wrote, she was sure she could sell it within weeks—that is, if he was willing to be treated financially as an "up and coming" author. He was. He was so willing in fact that he phoned immediately, whereupon a flattering secretary who actually knew who he was arranged an appointment for him on Thursday morning. An appointment to meet his agent! This occurrence drowned out all the noise of the world. The world that earlier was a din of discrimination and treachery was suddenly new. It was transformed. The agent had written that the novel, as he'd described the memoir, "might just be an important work of our time."

Let goddamn Bernardo Gallin do what he wants. His smug father too, for that matter. These were Adams's first thoughts, after he forced himself to think of what used to occupy him back in those dark, pre-agent days and hours that had just ended. Who was he to judge, he asked himself, what either of them did? Well, he could judge, but who was he to deliver the justice? In the end men did whatever they were meant to do. It was up to others, if they could, to avoid the trouble. Let someone else deliver justice. Adams suddenly had no time for aberrant pursuits or petty revenge. He was a writer. Success—the very prospect of it, the recognition of his talent—bled his anger. Let Bernardo Gallin have a new life, if he could live with himself. Let Richard Gallin wither in the one he was stuck with. It was far more important now that Adams find the proper tie for his momentous meeting, one that would clearly show his agent that this particular orphan was at least as much bon vivant as Artful Dodger now.

EXPERIMENTING FOR the first time in his life with calling in sick to work, Miguel was in a hurry that afternoon to get out of the apartment before his mother got back from work, and before his brother and young nieces came home from school. Mama's return

167

could come anytime after three, depending on which of her four employers she tended that day. Most days she returned around five. But she was usually later returning from her richest boss who, even though he lived alone, required more than the others. A trading desk manager, he was in the habit of half-shitting in his briefs during work. Maria, Miguel's mother, scrubbed and bleached them. He paid well, and had the decency to be embarrassed. "I'm sorry," he once said, seeing her scrubbing, "I should probably just buy new ones some weeks." He smiled weakly; she made no comment. But to Maria the notion was preposterous. When something was dirty you cleaned it. She'd had three babies. Shit didn't bother her. There was something gratifying about getting it out. She liked this man, in fact. They were about the same age. He seemed lonely in his big townhouse. She felt tender toward him when she thought about him sitting at his desk, watching a stock plummet, shitting himself.

But even though his mother's arrival was unpredictable, Miguel's brother and nieces would be back at three to sit in front of the television. They would tell Mama if they saw him home. There was never a reason to skip work in the Arellano family. Death excused, nothing less, the colonel always said.

Miguel stared into the bathroom mirror. He applied a yellow ointment to the holes in his ears and nose and lips. Then he took out the tube of white scar cream he'd ordered from television and rubbed it methodically onto the keloid on his cheek. He rubbed it with great concentration, as though trying to coax a genie from a bottle. Afterward, he washed his hands vigorously. No matter, they still felt greasy. He went into the room that he shared with his fat kid brother and slid a shoebox out from under the bed. It was a black Nike box, but Michael Jordan's silhouette was covered by a hundred red rubber bands that served as its unorthodox lock. He slid a key beneath the taut bands and yanked upward; they broke away easily. The bands were old. From the box he took the knife his father had given him after digging him out of the ground, a reward for his bravery. A symbol that meant he could do, could achieve, anything. He prized no possession more: the serrated steel blade five inches long and gleaming, the carved wooden hilt almost soft. He had shown it to no one in the nine years he'd been in this country. He looked at his face in the blade and then tucked it down into the back of his jeans, feeling the icy metal flat against the top of his ass. It felt good, erotic.

A new face and ten thousand dollars was his ticket, his invitation, to the America he saw on television. He was going to get it.

169

FIFTEEN

Peter's services secured, Gallin stepped sluggishly onto the bright street, his large heart overworked with love. Though he was bad at it, Gallin was a heavy lover of his fellow man. He loved in plump, grandiose bursts. Seeing the deaf, the old, the wheelchair-bound, the blind, a sunset, a puppy, a fiddler or an infant, he positively ached with emotion. With love and empathy. Also: the gin affected him.

He started uptown, but a strange force pulled at him, dragging on him like a second, horizontal, gravity. The best he could manage against it was a sideways move. Across the street, he bought Lifesavers at a newsstand. He'd catch a cab at 14th Street, he thought. Yet once more he was constrained, corralled. His thrusts signaled, his feet pointed, his eyes faced forward—but he slid back, like in Michael Jackson's moonwalk. It must be in my mind, he thought. And it was: the crater had a hold of him. Inside a cab he told the driver, "World Trade Center, please."

"You want go Ground Zero?" he said, staccato. "I have turn around."

The driver was Pakistani, Gallin guessed. It was another place he had been. Years before in Punjab, at a luncheon given for him on the magnificent patio of his hosts, a rich citrus-farming couple whose noses he'd resculpted, Gallin had watched a tiny bearded professor of literature perform extemporaneously the Lear monologue of madness from Act IV. It was a masterly performance. One which he had never seen the equal of on the stage. This small turban-wearing professor—Maini, was his name—in thick-lens glasses had become Lear, transformed before his eyes into all the royalty, agony and stupidity of the king. Gallin had since thought of Pakistan as a place of astonishing cultural wonders. He often told the story to Pakistani cab drivers, mimicking the professor through the taxi Plexiglas: *Fie, fie, fie! Pah! Pah!* He'd found over the years a surprising number of cabbies knew the play. But now he was not in the mood to regale. The heat in the cab blasted like a hair dryer's, it fired into his face; the smell of curry and onions floated on it, nauseatingly. Gallin, queasy, opened the window.

"Take Ninth Avenue," he choked out.

"No, sir. No Ninth Avenue. Ninth Avenue finished," the driver inclined his head only fractionally. "We take the highway."

He was right: Ninth Avenue ended farther uptown, the city's grid giving way to the capricious streets of Greenwich Village at 14th. In the village, 4th Street could, and did, intersect with 12th Street. Even lifelong New Yorkers, like Gallin, got turned around.

"The north side of the site, please."

"Ground Zero—the platform, you want. You go to the platform. But there is nothing to see," he said in a musical accent. "Only a big hole and millions of people go."

"Fine, the platform," Gallin responded.

The driver started speaking rapidly, laughing as he spoke. Gallin tried to follow until he realized the driver was talking on a cell phone. He popped another Lifesaver, pushing the tip of his tongue through the hole. Three blocks down they hit traffic. They crawled.

This traffic was odd, Gallin thought, for a reason he couldn't pinpoint. Then it struck him: no horns. He'd noticed an increased lawfulness among pedestrians since the attack. They seemed intent on giving up their small transgressions, like jay walking, as part of a yet-to-be-negotiated cosmic trade-off for restored world order. They waited patiently at lights to cross. It was good. But this silence from drivers he disliked. A reluctance to disturb, to push through, to sound out was—he was not sure if it was un-American but it was un-New York. Would it last? No sooner had he thought this than his cab got trapped in the middle lane of the West Side Highway, flagrantly blocking the box. The sore, retarded traffic inched around them. One horn blew. Then another. Then a tone-deaf symphony splintered his nerves. Be careful what you wish for, he thought.

A big Ford Explorer got held up in front of them. Its driver was in a rage, turning to the cabbie and giving him the finger. "Die you towel-headed bastard fuck," he screamed. "Go the fuck home."

Gallin saw that the Ford's bumper was plastered with half a dozen stickers that read "Never Forget." He'd seen this phrase a lot lately. It made him uncomfortable for it was such bad advice. Forgetting, he believed, was essential. It prevented constipation of the mind. There were things he longed very much to forget. An aperture appeared in the traffic, and the cab zipped through it onto Liberty Street.

As he drew closer, he saw the viewing platform that had been erected along the edge, and the line of people waiting hours to ascend it and gaze uncomprehendingly at the wreckage. Thousands thronged the site—nearly as many as had died there. Pale, grim families from god-knows-where stood morosely in this line inhaling lead-soaked dust and buying patriotic mementos. They were ghouls.

Gallin got out of the cab.

A Houlihan's restaurant that overlooked the platform had placed a placard outside that read: "Don't wait in the cold! You can see Ground Zero from our bar."

Gallin thought of the story of Jesus at the temple, turning over tables and dispatching the gold. That story had never seemed to fit with Christ's character. Indeed, Gallin always thought his rage a little ridiculous. Now, suddenly, he understood it. It was ridiculous *and* he understood it. He wanted to turn a few tables himself.

Yet for all his anguish over the spectacle, he understood that people sometimes needed to see a thing to make it real. These people on the platform might get a taste of metallic dust in their mouths and hold onto the sensation until the day they could forget it. Gallin looked up at the surrounding buildings, swaddled in giant black mesh jerseys that puffed out and back in soft waves from the wind. It looked as if the buildings breathed.

He needed to go. As he walked away he was moved by a group of young mothers who stood in the grisly line, babies harnessed to their chests. He couldn't understand what would compel a mother to bring her baby to this place. Why rush to introduce innocence to its conqueror? Yet somehow he trusted it. The mothers must know, he thought. Would these children, somehow, remember? Was that what Bernardo had meant about communicating something to Tyler? Just by holding him?

This place had been where his son had died, and now it wasn't. Now he didn't know what it was, except the most bizarre bazaar. He kept on walking.

He kept going far enough that Ana Garibaldi spotted him a half hour later, directly in front of her building on West 12th Street. He had strutted away his limp, militantly. Rhythm corrected things. When he walked by, Ana happened to be on her way to mail him a letter. She put little stock in coincidence or fortune—uncanny things rarely happened to her—but she had spent the better part of the last three hours putting her thoughts about Gallin and his collection down on paper; and here he went, strolling by, while she held those thoughts scripted in her hand. If there was bad luck, there must be the good kind, she thought. She wanted the job from him. The money would be terrific. But she was also ready to team up with someone. Ana was tired of loneliness. He was too, she could tell.

Gallin, who had no idea where Garibaldi lived, had made a right onto West 12th simply because its cobblestones were exposed. He was thinking about wisdom, and what made it. On the cobblestones, his mind turned to Ben Franklin. Bernardo had disparaged his "early to bed, early to rise" advice. But hadn't Franklin possessed superior wisdom? Gallin wondered if Franklin and Alexander Hamilton had gotten along. One invented the lending library and the other, the federal bank. Who was wiser?

"Richard," Ana called. "Richard Gallin."

He stopped and turned.

173

"Ana," he said, "I was just thinking about you." He lied.

"What are you doing down here? This is where I live, right here."

"I had to take care of some business—well, a business lunch. Forgive me, I'm out of sorts. You caught me by surprise. I was just thinking about Benjamin Franklin, I—"

"I thought you were thinking about me," she said teasingly.

"Yes, well I was. But the cobblestones for whatever reason made me think of Ben Franklin, and whether he got along with Alexander Hamilton."

"Oh, I think they hated each other," she said with gossipy charm. She smiled. "Despised each other," she said.

"I was going to call you," Gallin said.

"I would hope so. You hired me, remember?" She seemed to him so confident, so cool. She looked terrific, just in jeans and a sweater. "Would you like to come in for a minute? I actually have something for you. Two things. One is—oops, look at that—one is in my hand," she held out the envelope addressed to him. "But the other I couldn't just drop in the mail. It's a gift. Will you come up and let me give it to you? It'll be like a celebration of the coincidence of running into you."

"Well, I have to get going up to—"

"Or, now that I think of it, you could be stalking me. Are you stalking me, Dr. Gallin?" She was being cute, coy. She hoped he liked it.

"No, I've been stalked," he answered. "This is not that. This is just a lucky accident, I assure you."

"So you'll come up. I was just about to send you this letter, believe it or not. Just now."

"Really? May I have it then?"

"Well, now I'm a bit freaked out by running into you, and I wonder if I should just hang onto it—until I'm sure I mean what it says. I'd rather give you the gift, I think."

"You seem very sure of yourself to me, Ana."

The streetlamps flickered and then settled on light; the afternoon was finally ending. She handed him the letter. He glanced at his name rendered in her beautiful penmanship and slid the envelope into his inside pocket.

"Thank you."

"To be honest, I'm not sure if you're ready for what it says in there," she said, fire of the confessor lighting her face.

"Could we get a cup of coffee?" he asked.

"I can make some. Just like that," she said, and snapped her fingers and laughed.

"I'm sorry again, but I just want to be out now. You know when you want to be *in* the city?"

"Yes, of course I do, I—"

A strong wind blew from the west, tunneling onto them from Jane Street.

"My goodness, you're not wearing a coat and I'm standing here keeping you talking. Coffee," he said, and grabbed her by the elbow. He slinked out of half his overcoat with a shoulder contortion and then pulled off the rest and put it over her shoulders. It was enormous on her. She looked childlike in it.

"There's a Starbucks right there," she said without conviction.

"Is there anywhere else?" he asked.

The little café they chose smelled of baking dough, warm chocolate and French roast. They stood with their giant ceramic cups at the slim countertop by the front window. Gallin used his forearm to wipe away the condensation so they could see out onto the street. Two towers of light shot into the sky at the Trade Center site in the evenings. They were visible through the swatch Gallin cleared on the window. Dark had come on.

Gallin put his hand over his heart. "What does your letter say?" he asked.

"Oh, it's all awkward heartsong. The truth, I guess," she said. She warmed her hands over her cup. The sleeves of Gallin's coat dipped in.

"I don't know that I'm much versed in the truth," he replied. "I hope I can understand it. It may read like hieroglyphics to me." Gallin smiled. He was telling the truth in his favorite way, with the coat of sarcasm that made it sayable.

"I wish you had come up," she said. "You're really going to love what I got for you."

"I don't know why I didn't come up, honestly. I've got a lot on my mind and to be in your place, with you, I don't think I would've been able to think of any of it."

He reached for her hand, clasped it. It was the second time in three days that they held hands looking out a window. It seemed a tremendous accomplishment.

"You know I wanted to talk with you about what else is on your mind," she said. "God, I've wanted to talk to you about more things in the last two days than I can even think of. But I wanted to say that, you know, you can trust me, whatever you do. You can trust me no matter what."

Looking at the towers of light, beamed with such symbolic majesty through the sky, Gallin wondered if that wasn't the right and proper end for all material things, even lives when they ended, that they turn into light?

"I'm grateful for that," he said. "I'm sorry you were drawn into it."

"I'm glad I was. Or not glad, I hate that word, but I want to be where I am in it. Knowing. I feel like I can help. I understand what he's doing. I think it's honorable."

"You do? Honorable?"

"Oh, yes, I think it's brave. More brave than cowardly. More strong than weak. He was saying—I'm sorry, but I had to listen. He was saying 'wouldn't you do it, wouldn't you start again, Dad?' And I was thinking *YES!* It was like a question out of a great love story. Who wouldn't start over? Who wouldn't try it? It's like a great work of art. It's transformation. It's transformative."

"I keep going back and forth myself. As to what it is. The biggest decision I've made is that it doesn't matter what I believe, or think. It's not about my life. It's about Bernardo's. The strangest thing is that I had already thought he was dead, and what I find incomprehensible is that even now I think of him as dead. It's as if you can only die once—we can only process that once—and after that, even though I've hugged him and felt his breath on my face, he still seems dead to me. It's as if once you're dead you can't be anything else. It's like now he's a ghost. And so whatever the ghost does, who am I to say?"

"When are you going to do it?"

"The surgery? Tomorrow night is the plan."

She took a long slow sip of her café au lait.

"Is there anything I can do?"

"Oh, no. Well, besides that, I'll want company afterwards, I think. But that won't be until three in the morning probably."

"I can be there."

"He's only going to need twenty-four hours recovery time. And if I know Bernardo, he won't even take it. He was always a tough little kid, finding a way. I think he's planning to go the next night, but if he feels okay he'll surely slip out sooner. Under the knife will be the last time I may ever see him."

She squeezed Gallin's wrist.

"Ana, question. Do you think, I mean you only saw him the once—and I'll tell you he already looks very different from the way he looked before—but do you think he," Gallin hesitated, "looks like me?"

She sucked in her extravagant lips. Her smooth forehead pinched in the center and her yellow eyes looked down and away.

"Oh, no, you didn't even see him, that's right. You just heard us."

"Well, no, actually, I saw him. I looked out. I was afraid."

"Okay, well then you did see him? Did you think he looked like me?"

"I don't know," she said. "Why? Wait, yes he does. I was just remembering you when I first saw you, when we went to the Stanhope."

"He does, doesn't he? I never really saw it before. He seemed so different from me. He seemed so much more like his mother with those eyes. But when he came back I really saw it. And now I can't stop thinking about that part of it. His face looks so much like mine now in my mind's eye that I feel like I'm going to be operating on my own face."

"That is strange. Creepy."

"But it's not. You'd think so, but it's not. The creepiest part about the whole thing is what I'm supposed to do to it. What he's asking me to do is take a perfectly good face—not only a good face, but my face—and destroy it. I'm not trying to make him look better. I'm simply trying to make him look different. My whole life has been spent, whether you think it's a waste or not, trying to make people look more like who they really are—who they think they are inside."

"Hmmm, well I—" she said.

"Now I've got to do the opposite. Make him look like who he's not. It's more than just the ethical thing. As a practical matter, I don't know exactly how to do it. It's corrupt, corrosive. I mean I can feel already that it's going to cause me pain to do. And then on top of that it gets so strange when I see in him my own face."

"But you know it's not your face. Look at the way you described it, it's almost not even his face. It's a ghost's face. It's like a mask. You'll be making a mask. It's as though the animating spirit of his first mask, his old face, is used up, and he's got a new spirit that needs expression but no mask to speak through. You're just making what the spirit needs. An artist."

"That's good," he said. "That's interesting. It's smart as hell. It's intellectually stimulating. It's amazing what we can tell ourselves, amazing. But the things we can say as opposed to what we do ignores the blood. That nice clean spirit fix you describe is going to bleed a lot. Do you know how the face bleeds?"

"When my son was a baby he had stitches above his eye once, banged into a table, it was awful, but—"

"No, I mean blood where you have to cauterize the blood vessels. You pull the skin up and you singe them with an electric burner to make it stop. It sparks. You can see the sparks, and smell the burn. It goes fissst. Fissst."

"No, I don't know that."

178

"I just want to do the right thing. I've spent a good deal of my life not quite doing that. After my wife died I felt sorry for myself, I suppose, and then I wasn't really *there*, as they say, for Bernardo. I always felt rotten about it, but it truly haunted me when he died—or when I thought he was dead. You always think that whatever you've done badly you can make up for. Then, suddenly, time runs out and you can't.

"But then I find out he's *alive*. I get a second chance that nobody gets, right? Now I can be there for him. I'm in a position ultimately to help him get what he wants. But is it right? Now that you have the power, do you use it? It seems to me I have to do whatever I can. Because I did fail him as a father. I did fail him."

"You can't say that," Ana interrupted, gravely. "You can't. You can only give, as a human being, what's available to you. My husband—I don't think he failed our son and my husband killed himself. But my son has many of his father's gifts. Bernardo must have some of yours too. That's not a failing."

"And my problems, he's probably got."

"Yours and his own."

"You know, I became a plastic surgeon because I wanted to make people feel good. The world seemed so goddamn antagonistic toward people. Just plain mean, really. Understand, this was when I was much younger. But all the doctors I studied with were basically trying to make people die slower. That's an oversimplification, but it's true. That's the objective of medicine when you think about it—to make people die slower. And I wanted to see if I could make people live happier. Have a better quality of life. Sounds clichéd, I know. You may think a breast augmentation is a strange way to achieve a better life. You may think it's pathetic. But it works. You're beautiful, Ana. You've never needed any help for the world to see that. But other people do. People are miserable inside their skin. Maybe it's a mental defect and they should be able to feel better without changing their appearance, I don't know. But the fact is they don't feel better. And it's the case with too many people to call it a defect. If more than half of human beings feel a certain way, how can we say what they feel is a defect? Isn't that more like design?

"But I'm not sure it's been valuable, what I've done with my life. I can point to thousands of examples of improved lives, thousands, but I wonder if the cumulative effect has been positive. If I haven't just contributed to the shallowness of the culture."

"It's probably some of both," she said.

But Gallin didn't really hear her answer. He was thinking back to a woman he saw as he canvassed downtown in the first days after the attack, posting photos of Bernardo on any surface available, where his face took its tiny place among the masses of missing. He could not forget her. Wherever he went that day, she followed. She carried around a big nylon laundry bag filled with her husband's shoes. She left them scattered around with notes in them, believing that if the man was somehow alive and wandering the area in a daze, he might recognize his own shoes and read the notes in them that said *come home.*

SIXTEEN

On Tuesday evening Miguel spotted Adams easily, making his way down 7th Avenue with two department store tote bags in the clutch of one long pendulous arm. He was just as Gallin had described him, though he exceeded that description in the consummate gaiety of his stride, which was like that of a sprinter but in slow motion, knees high, arms jabbing. He seemed to sing, too, beneath his breath. His head bobbed to some internal music and his lips moved with lewd concupiscence, revealing the edges of his brilliantly white teeth. At intervals, he smiled to his left or right at nothing more than a felicitous movement of the air, sometimes stopping to gaze into a store window, lured at first by some item but then mesmerized by his own reflection. Twice in three blocks he adjusted his tie in a window, black leather gloves fidgeting with a thick crimson knot, his self-regard palpable. In the window of an eyeglasses store he actually winked at himself and then, as if in an apology for misusing the glass, gave the frames on display a full minute's worth of ardent consumer scrutiny. He moved along.

Miguel found himself drawn to this peculiar figure. Technically speaking, Adams was ugly. His face was a freckled, lopsided three-quarter moon, his hair a rusted metallic thicket. But he exuded joy, and style. He even managed to appear taller than he was; he walked the avenue as though he wore a top hat. A cane would not have been out of place. Yet except for Adams's being white—and what a poor white to be, Miguel thought, pale and freckled and red—Miguel saw that his own shortcomings were no graver than Adams's. Miguel recognized in Nick the magic trick he had always imagined performing himself—how with the

181

suit and the confidence Adams overcame how he looked. How he turned the tables. Both women and men looked at him as they passed, slowing down and forgetting the cold to investigate his strange, attractive effect. Their eyes petted him. This was not the way they looked at Miguel, which was fearfully. They looked at Adams hungrily, imbibing him. It was fun to look, to watch him move.

Miguel regarded his own reflection in the window of a card store. Could he pull it off? He could, he thought. He just needed the clothes, the money. He needed the scars removed from his face. As it was, no one could see him properly. He was camouflaged. His own clothes were, he saw even more conspicuously in this neighborhood, the contemporary uniform of the urban poor, no matter how expensive: black jeans, white t-shirt, black Northface jacket, Adidas sneakers. But it was all so easy to change! Like Adams, he stopped in front of the window that showed the eyeglasses. Though his vision was perfect—he had been the best marksman at the Nicaraguan camp—he planned to get glasses to go along with his suits. All the people in the window posters—and there was a handsome Latino, too—had these extraordinary eyes. The glasses showed them off. Once near the end of high school, a pretty girl in his class had told Miguel that his beige eyes were beautiful. Beautiful, she'd said. She said he had the long eyelashes of a dreamer. It was a shame, she said, about his face.

Enjoying Adams's triumphal gait, seeing the redhead as an example of what he might achieve, Miguel started to wish that it were some other character he was going to have to handle. But when Adams entered at the address Gallin had given, there could be no mistake: this was his man. Miguel hung around the neighborhood, getting a hot dog at the Papaya King. Later he watched Adams and Peter have dinner in a small corner restaurant called Chez Michellet. It was the kind of place Miguel pictured himself in, with a beautiful girl, the interior bronze and warm, the glasses glowing red with wine, the dance of candlelight. He imagined the music inside: rich and melodic, the opposite of the tinny spastic Puerto Rican rhythms that jangled ceaselessly throughout his own building. When Peter and Adams emerged from the restaurant, they looked incredibly happy. They held hands. Miguel was surprised. That they were having a romantic dinner hadn't occurred to him; he'd been too busy eating his own meal vicariously through them, trading places in his mind. But he had nothing against gays. In fact, he felt sympathy for them because in his country they used to torture them, especially in the militia. If one was found out in camp, he was sodomized with a burning branch. It made Miguel squirm now to think about it. He'd watched his father do it once, to a boy Miguel had liked, the son of one of his mother's friends. The colonel had stuffed the burning branch into him until the red ember was snuffed out between the skinny cheeks of his bony ass. That boy, Angel, had run away. He was probably dead. Miguel felt a little sick, thinking about Angel. He put him out of his mind.

He followed the hand-holding couple surreptitiously until they crossed 14th Street, trying to determine if Adams was really a boxer, whether he was going to be much trouble. He knew at least not to underestimate him because he was gay. One of the boys who'd got the burning branch in his ass had later cut off the balls of the soldier who stuffed him. Cut them off while he was sleeping and hung them from a tree limb.

At 14th Street Miguel went down into the harsh light of the subway station, through a corridor rife with defiled advertising posters where the models' teeth were all blackened. Get insurance, get good hair, have a cognac, see a movie. At the magazine stand on the middle level, hundreds of slick covers glared in the fluorescence featuring big black asses in thong bikinis, rappers draped in chains, topless white teenagers in cheerleader skirts and ponytails, smiling Salt Lake gold medalists, self-proclaimed prince of darkness Ozzy Osbourne, darkness itself Osama bin Laden, French-made Israeli tanks and American-made Oprah. So many magazines.

He went down another flight to the platform. Rats scampered across the tracks. He wondered how many people ate them. They ate pigeons, he knew, but nobody admitted to eating the rats. Maybe no one did. There were eighty people, he guessed, waiting for trains. Everyone carried a bag—a briefcase, a computer satchel, a Macy's bag, something. Some carried two or three. Miguel was the only one on the platform empty-handed. He wondered what everyone carried. What was so important to them? The number 3 train careened in, the sound of screeching steel forcing the sensitive to put their fingers in their ears. Miguel could see almost everyone at once. It was something you learned in the jungle. No one seemed to notice him though, which was good.

Across the platform he picked out a group of five coming down the stairs, wearing the same thing he was. They were noticed: you could see the wariness in people's quick glances, the stiffening of bodies, the subtle moving away. None of these five had a bag either. They were laughing and shouting, saying "Damn nigger" this and "damn nigger" that, punching each other with great force in the arms. The word nigger echoed from the concrete ceiling. Two of them wore do-rags, which made Miguel check quickly for colors, but these weren't gangbangers, he determined, just kids fucking around. They were in the uniform, his uniform, and played a little rougher from having less space to play in. Alone though, someone like him drew little attention. For now that was good. He would come back down here in a few months and people would be looking at him differently, the way they looked at Adams walking down the street. But for now it was good to go unnoticed.

It was later than he thought when he got home. The apartment was dark. In his bedroom he put the knife quietly under his pillow and stripped to his briefs. The ancient radiator hissed and clicked, its paint peeling off; the pipes clanged as though someone on another floor was striking them with a hammer. His mother and brother would sleep through it. They slept through any commotion, the boy catatonic with calories and the woman weary from work. His little brother's big round head lay tenderly on the pillow, his small mouth open, his sugared lips crusty from the heat. Even with the windows half-open, the apartment was stiflingly hot, and dry. Miguel grazed the boy's shoulder affectionately, with no fear that he would wake.

He dropped to the floor and pumped out fifty push-ups, smoothly sliding up from them to kneel at his bedside. He whispered his prayers. Miguel was certain that Jesus knew him and listened to him pray. One hundred more push-ups followed, sharp military snaps. His arms burned pleasingly and he turned over, ripping off a hundred-and-fifty sit-ups. The last looked identical to the first. He was a physical machine. He drank a glass of water in the kitchen and then lay in bed thinking of some of the great fights he'd seen—camp skirmishes, street brawls, boxing matches. That punch the other night on TV though, the one that killed that guy in Atlantic City, was the most devastating. He played it over and over again in his mind, picturing himself throwing it, until he drifted into an arid sleep.

The next night, Wednesday, just after eight o'clock, five days after selling Gallin a pair of shoes at the Foot Locker, Miguel slit Adams's throat in Central Park, having tailed him for almost sixty blocks through Chelsea's charm, midtown's grit, right up through Central Park South's nostalgic horse-manure-scented glamour. The park, for all its civil niceties, was also a wilderness and offered vast opportunity. To Miguel's astonishment, his mark had walked directly in and started winding crosstown on a dark unpopulated path. He was unsure until the moment it happened. Only when he felt himself switching to long silent strides to overtake him did Miguel realize he would do it, like the marathoner who suddenly sees his moment to break from the pack. The action was swift and neat, a diagonal cut from jaw to clavicle. With his free hand he took Adams by the waist and guided his enervated body down onto an adjacent bench as though it were a woman's, fainted. Adams never spoke, had no opportunity to resist. Miguel used great skill to avoid his blood.

185

It was only the second time he had taken a life. The first had been unambiguous, a matter of survival. He was proud of that one. But killing Adams seemed terribly trivial. There had been so much death lately. It was, literally, overkill.

Guilt worked on him like a heavy bag, and the fifth commandment echoed in his ears. But he countered its echo with his own, repeating to himself what he had long ago learned about killing: that he did only what had to be done. It was a mantra, substituted for reason. You had to force the future's hand. Miguel failed to consider that perhaps this was meaningless, that nothing fit this description. That nothing, actually, had to be done. But Miguel had risen out of the world where imperatives were more easily, matter-of-factly conceived. He wasn't schooled in uncertainty, but black and white. You had food or you didn't; you had enemies or friends. In that world *it had to be done* was a rationale for all sorts of depravity. Besides, invented imperatives were tricky. It was the only way things got done. Without imperatives we would have no vaccines, no art, and no airplanes. But also, of course, no war, no rape, and no murder.

He placed his soft-hilted knife in Adams's right hand and watched it fall to the ground. It would be a strange-looking suicide—exceptionally brutal, gruesome. But people were generally so disturbed now that it wouldn't be unbelievable. Plus the NYPD wouldn't want a killer loose, not with the load on its plate already. The cops would say it was suicide, surely, given the chance.

IN GALLIN'S operating room, the twin halogen bulbs affixed on spring-elbowed arms stuttered nervously toward illumination before firing light and heat up into the polygon reflecting domes that hooded them, producing two cool incandescent cylinders that beamed down onto the empty surgical table. This sectoring of the light—that it was fractured by the domes into a thousand separate pieces—assured that it cast no shadows. Gallin, feeling strangely happy, could not remember the last time he'd prepared his own surgery. Flipping on these beams and spotting them in place, he was reminded of one of the phrases that had attracted him when he'd begun: the surgical theatre. Spotlights, drama, players, weapons, hopes, fears, blood, suction, something changed—it was romantic, the theatre. Flitting around the O.R. now, taking care of pre-op duties that normally fell to his nurse, Gallin felt a reassuring sense of thoroughness. It was not unlike exhilaration. The small details that in professional maturity one could delegate, he thought, the loss of these was a terrible, fragmenting loss. We were so highly specialized now. We knew so little about how anything around us, the things we counted on, worked. Did one percent of drivers understand the engine, talkers the phone, watchers the television? He lined the table with fresh paper. Gallin lovingly placed his instruments—retractors, forceps, scissors, scalpels, all coruscating steel—into a blue foam pouch and dropped them into the steaming autoclave for sterilization. This thoroughness, was this religion?

The phone in his office jingled: he heard distantly the unique double-ring it made to indicate the door. He looked at his watch, the one that was stolen and miraculously returned. It was Peter, right on time. But where was Bernardo? Perhaps he's changed his idiot mind! But as Gallin removed his white coat to go downstairs and admit Peter, Bernardo appeared like an apparition in front of him. He moved so silently now. His appearance was startling. His scruffy beard was gone and his head was shaved completely clean—now a white helmet gruesomely topped his tanned face. He looked alien, a weird animal, some pharaonic admixture of man and ram. His skinniness, his two-toned head, the white shaven part seeming unnaturally distended, made a revolting picture. Seeing it, Gallin felt a polluted wave come up in his stomach. He threw his arms in grief around the boy. But Bernardo was stoic.

"That's him, right?" he asked, meaning the double-ringing. "Peter?"

Gallin thought of Abraham and Isaac. Was he making a sacrifice? Was this a test? Would he be relieved?

"Bernardo, you haven't eaten—correct, son?"

"No, sir, I haven't."

"You look weak."

"I feel strong."

"Okay, sit. Sit. Take a seat on the table. I have to let Peter in. But let me ask you now, are you sure you want to do this? There are other ways out, simpler, more honest ways."

"Honest? Are you kidding me? Honest?"

"Okay, you know what I'm talking about—"

"I do. I'm sorry, Dad," he interrupted. "I am sure. I really am."

His eyes were clear and placid in his deranged-looking skull. "Please don't think too much about this. You're doing the right thing. You're doing what has to be done, you know? I've dealt the cards—or Bin Laden or God or somebody dealt them. It's in motion. Just treat it like it's anybody else, any other day."

"I'll have to."

"Thank you."

"I'll be right back," Gallin said. He touched Bernardo's shoulder, and walked downstairs.

Bernardo picked up a blanket next to the table and lay down, covering himself around the shoulders. He stared into the halogen suns until his eyes couldn't stand it and then he closed them, watching the flecks of memorized light fly across the backs of his eyelids like a meteor shower.

Opening the door downstairs, Gallin was surprised. With Peter was also Ana. Gallin saw the white puffs containing their last words to each other float off in the dark; he wondered what the words were.

"Hello," Gallin said cheerfully. "Hello to you both. Ana, I didn't expect you until much later. Come in, come in both of you. Out of the cold."

Inside, Ana said, "I can come back."

"No, no, it's fine. It's wonderful. I assume you've met, introduced yourselves?"

They both nodded.

"Yes, Peter blocked the wind for me," Ana said.

"Good. Come in. I'll take you upstairs. Peter, if you don't mind waiting, I'll drop you at my office. The patient's in the O.R. now— I ask that you not go in there till we've spoken. I've done some of the prep already. In fact, I have a renewed appreciation for it."

"I'll wait wherever you wish, Dr. G."

Gallin saw Ana look up at Peter. She liked him instantly, his heavy lids and blue eyes, his softness.

The elevator stopped on the second floor and Peter got off. "Just have a seat in the office, Peter. Please, I'll be just a minute."

When the elevator door shut, Ana kissed Gallin flush on the lips. She wore flats and had to lean up to do it. The toeing made her feel girlish, free. Coming here she felt like she was entering a secret world.

"What are you doing here?" Gallin asked, and quickly added, "I mean I'm very glad you're here, but we'll be hours before we finish."

"I'll wait," she replied, smiling. "Read a book or something. Same thing I'd do somewhere else but near you. I hoped it would be good for us. Besides, if I'm going to catalogue your collection based on who you are, I'll need to snoop around." She smiled again. "Keep things light where possible."

The elevator opened on the fifth floor.

"I wish the dogs were here," Gallin said wistfully, pulling her out by the hand. "Keep you company. You'd love Baby, sweetest dog in the world. Barney's a little more grouchy. But he was abused as a puppy. I rescued him, really. He's still not over it. What am I talking about?"

"What you care about. That's natural," Ana said.

"You have a lot of answers, you know? That makes me very suspicious," he grinned. "I used to have them all."

"It comes and goes," she said, and kissed him again.

"Peter," Gallin half-roared as he entered his office. "Peter, I'm so glad you could do this. No, no sit, have a seat again."

189

Gallin himself sat.

"Peter, first of all, here is a bag with ten-thousand dollars in it."

He handed over a plain black plastic bag that you might get a bottle of wine in. It was unsealed and stuffed with cash.

"Now," he continued, "there's something else. You remember we talked about discretion?" Gallin put another plastic bag on his desk. This one was blue, a shield for a rainy day newspaper, fastidiously secured by a dozen rubber bands. "This is something extra, an extra five-thousand. It's for you. It's from the patient and it's meant as a kind of extra security—or extra reward—for your discretion. In other words, your total silence."

"Wow," said Peter, staring at the blue bag.

"You can go ahead and take it now, put it in the bag you brought with you."

"It's amazing."

"Okay, I'm going to go in and give the IV. You can get scrubbed in just a few minutes, but first stay here a moment so we can talk. I'll be right back."

Gallin felt something like a cold arrow pierce him as he crossed the threshold from his office, hyper-civilized with its books, globes and rich carpet, into the clinical milieu of the O.R., built for action with its white-cum-metal minimalism, its tubes and machines, its shadowless light. *Epistêmê* versus *technê*, Gallin thought. In one room we think, in the other we do. He turned on the music. Gallin always operated while listening to WQXR, the classical music radio station. It was the last station of its kind, a beautiful survivor. During the last few months especially it had been a small miracle, showing over and over what humans could do. He loaded the syringe and tapped Bernardo, who opened his eyes. Gallin injected the IV sedation into a large violet vein in his left arm, swabbing it before and after, taping cotton to it. Most of his facial surgery was done this way: an IV sedation first, combining morphine and valium, inducing what was called twilight sleep, then a series of locals to deaden the immediate nerves.

190

"Are you ready?" he asked Bernardo. "For me to bring Peter in?"

"What did you tell him?"

"Nothing yet. Only that the 'patient' wanted him to have this extra five-thousand dollars for his discretion."

"So he doesn't know it's me? Will he recognize me, do you think?"

Gallin squinted at his son. The forearm where he had put the needle was pumped and tight, his bicep hard. But the shaved globular dome of his two-toned head made his brownish face look petite and sucked in. Gallin himself hardly recognized him. But Peter would. Gallin remembered that Peter would sometimes comment, looking at a picture, about how handsome Bernardo was.

"Yes, he'll know who you are. First of all, he's going to come in here dying to know who you are. You're some kind of giant mystery already, and now you're a giant mystery who just gave him five-thousand dollars for what he was set to do anyway."

"You think I shouldn't have given—"

"If I thought that, I wouldn't have. I'm just saying he's going to know. But I'll say this too: the only people who know who you are—or that you're alive—are in this house now. Ana is upstairs and Peter's fifty feet away. I think you're safe with that being the case. In fact, I find it remarkable it's so small a group. And this guy Adams may or may not know. There's nothing anyway he can be sure about. But if you want to change your mind, Bernardo, do it now. Nothing has happened yet that's irreversible."

"No," Bernardo said, and closed his eyes. The valium was moving through him.

"You might keep those eyes of yours closed and it's possible he won't recognize you. Possible."

"Okay. Hey, I thought you said you were doing something about the Adams guy."

"Well, yes, but I don't know what I'm doing about it really. I just don't know if he's significant enough to be a real problem."

"Okay," Bernardo said.

191

Peter recognized Bernardo right away. It was evident in his face, which twitched, and in the way he ground his teeth harder than usual. He was confused. But he chose silence, deciding to say only what was necessary. In life, he'd found this was a very satisfactory strategy in dealing with surprise, or disappointment. Others talked too much.

"Sir," Peter said to Bernardo, "This is going to hurt a little bit. Sort of a pinch, a sting. But only for a second. After that you won't feel anything."

Peter injected Bernardo's two cheeks from the inside, pricking the pink gummy walls repeatedly, covering an inch square on each.

Bernardo flinched a couple of times.

"Peter," Gallin pronounced, "the patient is going to get a chin and jaw implant in addition to the cheeks. After that we're going to take some cartilage from behind the ear and build up a lump of sorts into the bridge of the nose. The patient's objective is not to look more attractive, in a traditional sense, but simply to look less like he does at present. Indeed, the patient would like to look like a different person."

Bernardo, groggy, said, "Dad, you don't have to call me *the patient*." His speech was clear, but deliberate. He was feeling the soulful grace of morphine. "Peter knows who I am. Or who I was. And Peter, you don't have to keep calling me 'sir.'"

"Okay, Bernardo," Gallin said. "That's enough. You relax now. It doesn't make a difference to Peter who you are. You're a patient, he's a professional. That's the whole story. It's all we're concerned with here today."

But of course it wasn't even a portion of the story. Not an inkling of it. Not a smidgen. But what could he say? Before he'd felt like Abraham, and now he felt like Frankenstein.

"Peter, I want to thank you," Bernardo started. "I know this must seem strange to you. But my father says you are a good man, a genuinely good man, and true to your word. I thank you for that. All I can say is that I'm doing what's necessary for me—"

"Bernardo, that's enough," Gallin said. Now he wants to talk?

"No, listen," Bernardo continued, the glow from the drugs in his voice. "I had the life, right? Peter, you know what that means? I *made* it. What they don't tell you is that once you make it you have to keep making it, you know? They don't tell you that you have to keep liking it. That every day no matter what the life you've got is, you've got to like it all over again. And again and again. Once you get it, it's supposed to be easy."

"Bernardo, take it easy now," Gallin said.

"I feel sick."

Bernardo lurched to his side, his head cast over the side of the table.

"Did you give him the Droperidol?" Peter asked.

"Oh Jesus, I forgot. Bernardo, hold on. You'll feel better, just one second. Peter, grab—"

But Peter had already grabbed a fresh syringe, filled it quickly with the anti-nausea drug and was shooting it into Bernardo's arm, right where Gallin had injected him.

"What else did you give him—for the pain, I mean?" Peter asked.

"Twenty milligrams valium, seven and a half morphine."

"Okay. There now, Bernardo," Peter said, sweet, lumpy-voiced. "It's fine now, you're fine now. The nausea will go away in a minute. Can you sit up?"

"Yesth."

"Okay, good, now lie back down here and just relax."

Bernardo spouted: "You realize people would kill to get what I had!"

"Bernardo!" Gallin said brusquely. "We're going to stop this. We're not going to do this."

Patient reluctance, Gallin thought. It used to be a sign to look for, a red flag, something that meant *stop*. That was when his career began. Later it was something for the surgeon to surmount. Patient reluctance was just nerves, cowardice. A patient got no credit for being rightly reluctant. The point where a decision had to be final was before they were on the table.

193

"No, do it, please, continue. I was just telling Peter that they would—people would kill. In case he had any doubts about my future. He could think about that—how I really must have needed to do this. How I had what people would kill for and gave it up."

Peter said nothing, was all solemn professionalism.

"I'm not going to ask you again if you're sure, Bernardo," Gallin said, "but I am going to need to ask you to stop talking. I'm going to do your cheeks first and I need your mouth to be still. We can't—work while you're talking."

Gallin would normally begin a combination procedure like this with chin and jaw. But he wanted to get his personal bearings, and the cheeks through the mouth was a better place to start. Bernardo had done him a favor in shaving his head: Gallin felt less that he shared the same face with his son, so alien did the boy look with his skull all tonsured and white. But still it would be easier to start in the mouth because with the chin, he'd have to cut from the outside, through the skin, if only a sliver of an incision. He'd have to look him right in the face for that.

Okay, here goes, he thought. And as Peter held the mouth open, Gallin cut a pocket inside large enough to push the implant through. The mouth demanded special care because of all the parts of the body that were regularly exposed, the mouth loved infection most. It craved it. Blood bothered neither Gallin nor Peter, of course. They had on numerous occasions discussed what to order for lunch while a patient's blood leaked all over their hands and clothes. Peter had tossed hundreds of pounds of sucked-out human fat into a bucket while considering the leanness of the pastrami at a nearby deli. Nevertheless, the mouth presented a heightened concern, as staunching flow there was sometimes harder and the patient should not be allowed to swallow his blood. It always happened, but they strived for patients to swallow as little as possible. Peter had the suction hose in Bernardo's mouth, working like a miniature maid. His other two fingers pressed on

Bernardo's molars, top and bottom, creating as large a work area for Gallin as he could. His thick fingers were an advantage here for their strength, but their size was sometimes problematic. Two hands were a lot to have in one mouth.

The first implant went in easily, and Gallin, in a laborer's groove, let his mind float away on the wings of the music. Surgery was like that—like golf or sex or dancing—in that you could think about other things while you did it. These wings were strapped to Beethoven's Ninth Symphony, a favorite, a testament. But the music was the opposite of how he now felt.

"Suction, please. Thank you."

The second symphonic movement rose up; Gallin felt revivified in its swell. It occurred to him that music was created out of tension, pressure on the air.

One hand in and one out, he pushed the little silicone implant up into place, exaggerating the cheekbone. He did this mostly by feel. It would not make Bernardo more handsome, but it would change him. Gallin considered for a moment whether it wouldn't be better to do only one side. Asymmetry was the great trickster: it kept the onlooker off balance. The eye craved symmetry. But the effect would be greater still with a second implant. He would place it differently, lower perhaps, creating an even more disjointing asymmetry—and at the same time enlarging the face.

He really ought to sell the townhouse, he thought, as the third movement began. If he simply sold it, got a nice apartment, his money troubles would be over.

Inside the mouth again, he started to cut before Peter was quite ready. Trying to catch up, Peter lost his grip on the suction and it dove to the back of Bernardo's throat. He bit down, gasping for air. And when he bit, Gallin's scalpel sliced across Peter's thick thumb, plunging through the latex into the skin. Peter tried to pull it out, but Bernardo's jaw clenched. It took less than three seconds for Peter to withdraw his bleeding thumb from Bernardo's mouth. But it was an infinite three seconds, with his blood dripping into Bernardo's mouth. He stared at Gallin in horror. Behind his mask his mouth hung open.

195

"Suction, suction," Gallin yelled, his voice dry as though it too were being suctioned, but there was nothing, really, to suck. "Damn it. Goddamn it. Goddamn it. Jesus," he said.

SEVENTEEN

The phone's ring slipped the real world and entered Gallin's dream. The dream adjusted. It cast the ringing as a school bell in the story it had underway, the last school bell in the spring of 1949 that released an eight-year-old boy into a long summer's sweltering whimsy. That summer, he would learn to swim. He woke. It was phenomenal: dreams appeared to be self-contained, interior, and yet they borrowed from the actual. The mind was so powerful, had so many tricks. We knew almost nothing about it. Why would the mind expose itself?

The ringing persisted. Gallin climbed out of bed to answer but it stopped. Good. The smell of coffee wafted in. Ana was brewing it. What time was it? Nine-thirty. What day was it? Thursday, but it took a moment. He twisted a wand, and the long blinds flexed open. Sunlight flushed in. The slatted sky was blue, cloudless. He needed to tell Bernardo what had happened.

The ringing began again, and though he knew it was nonsensical, Gallin sensed urgency in it. He let it ring.

"Ana," he called.

"In here, Richard," she replied, sounding busy at something. "There's coffee."

"Okay."

After a dozen rings he picked up the phone.

"Hello."

Nothing. No reply. He could hear that someone was on the other end—ambient clatter—but no voice answered him.

"Listen," he barked into the phone. "I don't know how you got this number. I had it changed. But if you call here again, or show up here again, I really will make trouble for you. Do you hear me?"

"Richard," a woman's voice said suddenly.

"Oh, I'm sorry. Who's this?"

"Richard Gallin? Dr. Richard Gallin?"

"Yes, goodness, I'm sorry. Who is this please?"

"Richard," said the trembling voice. "This is Cicely Rhodes. I wanted to call you myself."

"Oh, no."

"Yes, I'm afraid. Yes," her voice caught, snagged on love. He heard her work for air. "He left us yesterday just after two o'clock. He went peacefully. Put himself in his pajamas. He knew, Richard."

"Cicely, I'm so sorry."

"He was so happy to have seen you. He kept talking about it, saying how fit you looked. He said when you were together it was as though the years peeled back for him. That's what he said, 'peeled back.'"

Gallin wondered whether Rhodes had told her he'd mowed him down, bloodied him.

"It was special for me, too. He was a strong man, a great man to me. The world is worse off."

"Nothing could be more true," Cicely Rhodes replied, and Gallin sensed that she too left the world a little just then.

In the living room, Ana was sitting on the sofa looking at the masks and making notes when Gallin entered. "One of my heroes died," he told her.

Ana looked up. She had a generous way of expressing empathy with her eyes.

"Who was that?" she asked. "Your hero?"

"An older man, a doctor, named Rhodes. A friend."

"I'm very sorry."

"He had a full life, I think."

IN HIS robe he descended through the empty house to the basement. The last stairs creaked. His feet were bare. The subterranean cold rose in his nose.

198

But Bernardo wasn't there. A note on lined schoolboy loose-leaf paper lay on the table. "Dear Dad," it read. "I love you. Bernardo."

Gallin put it in his pocket. There was a chance he wouldn't get sick. There was a good chance, in fact. Bernardo was smart. He would see a doctor. If it happened, he would discover it. It was treatable. Life goes on. That was what you learned. Life went on, until it didn't.

As he made his way back up, he heard someone buzzing at the door. *Closed*, he wanted to say. He wanted to hang a sign on the front door, dangling from a little chain, like they did at restaurants. "No nourishment, no atmosphere. No pleasure here today."

Not this hour.

Not available.

He picked up an extension in his waiting room. It would answer the outside world through a speaker.

"I'm sorry," he announced, "The office is closed today."

"But I am here," came the simple reply.

Gallin recognized Miguel's voice.

"Doctor, it's you," he said, "I can hear. And I am here now."